PRAISE FOR
Heat Lightning

" Ruth Coe Chambers' gutsy protagonist Anna Lee Owens returns to Bay Harbor in this post WWII novel, where soldiers come home with souvenirs and heartache. Chambers navigates the squalls as bad things happen to her characters, and people fall in and out of love, inflicting harm thoughtlessly and deliberately. Through it all, young Anna Lee sees past the pitfalls and spite of small town life. She grows up, but keeps her humor and her love for Bay Harbor. *Heat Lightning* is a moving read you'll be sad to see end."

— *Carol Costello, WRITE IN THE ZONE blogger and author of*
Chasing Grace: A Novel of Odd Redemption

"Anna Lee Owens lives in post-WWII Bay Harbor, a town that has a way of making its residents believe they are more important than they are. Anna Lee takes them on, struggling with the forces of love and death, truth and deceit. *Heat Lightning* is an enthralling read, and Ruth Coe Chambers has created in Anna Lee a character you won't soon forget."

— *Adair Lara, writing coach and author of*
Naked, Drunk and Writing

PRAISE FOR
The Chinaberry Album

" . . . Ruth Coe Chambers uses Anna Lee's point of view artfully as she explores the
terror of growing up in a world full of conflicting rules and values . . ."

The New York Times Book Review

" . . . Ruth Chambers has created a delicious period piece,
full of the authentic flavor of the deep South."

Rosemary Daniell, author of
Fatal Flowers: On Sin, Sex, & Suicide in the Deep South

" . . . Chambers proves a deft writer who . . . can summarize
an entire way of life in a few words . . ."

In Pittsburgh

" . . . Indeed, the author keeps deepening character right to
the last sentence, one that will bring tears to the eyes of many readers—
well-earned tears, not cheap ones."

Fort Lauderdale News/Sun-Sentinel

" . . . Bright and sensitive story . . . pleasant excursion . . .
into the atmosphere of its time and place."

Kirkus Reviews

". . . Chambers has the relaxed-as-molasses ability to make
Bay Harbor and its inhabitants come alive . . ."

The Fresno Bee

Heat Lightning

Ruth Coe Chambers

Secluded Cove Press

Heat Lightning
First Edition

Copyright © 2013 Ruth Coe Chambers

Published by Secluded Cove Press

Print
ISBN-13: 978-0-9890109-2-4
ISBN-10: 0-9890109-2-9

Printed in the United States of America
10 9 8 7 6 5 4 3 2 1

Cover design and layout by Mica McPheeters

DEDICATION

Heat Lightning is dedicated with love to Bill Quarles,
my childhood pal and adult friend, without whose inspiration and kindness
this book would not have been written.

Acknowledgements

I can't express enough gratitude to Mica McPheeters and Belinda Hulin for all their work in giving *Heat Lightning* a place of its own in the Bay Harbor Trilogy.

PROLOGUE

Had they not left, Anna Lee would be starting high school in Bay Harbor soon, and she was frightened by the prospect of a strange school where she didn't know anybody. There were dark circles under red rimmed eyes, but she couldn't do anything about that. It was the nightmares. They began after they moved to Tallahassee. Every night she fought to stay awake, knowing what waited beyond sleep.

Hilton Fields' car eased into town quiet as a dream, dark as a hearse. It was late, and the streets of Bay Harbor were deserted. Fog crept in from the Gulf of Mexico and dimmed his headlights with webs of angel hair. Hilton was coming back from the dead. No, that wasn't it. World War II had ended, and Hilton, lean and fit, perfect as a mannequin, was coming to see his closest friend, Robert Owens. He smiled at the thought.

Robert and his wife, Estelle, were asleep, but their young daughter, Anna Lee, was awake, listening for the car. She knew Hilton had arrived, and she had to stop him before he reached their house. Still in her nightgown, she ran out the front door on dream-weighted feet. "Stop," she tried to shout, but the dream choked her. "Oh, please stop."

She always woke up with her face wet with tears, one word on her lips. Stop.

CHAPTER
One

Post World War II – 1940s

The tea colored water of the bay eased back and forth over seaweed and sand lapping at Bay Harbor's toes. Farther up the Florida coast the Gulf drew the town to its embrace with the titan force of undertow after a storm.

The townspeople took the water for granted, had long since grown accustomed to the quiet brilliance of sunsets that slid beneath the bay and the promise of buoyancy from the briny water of the Gulf. They wore its fragile mist on their skin, breathed the scent of it, and tasted the salt as it rode the wind. The water defined the people and the town. Barrier or gate.

Despite the sparkling waters and the picture perfect sunsets, Bay Harbor wasn't a picture postcard town. It had that lived-in look. Cracked uneven sidewalks, a few businesses that could have used a coat of paint, the ramshackle Bay pier in desperate need of repair—flaws, but nothing hopeless. The main street was as unassuming as a dirt path. It didn't border the beach, had no claim to beauty but remained sun washed and treeless, a road straight to the heart with a complete lack of pretense that made Bay Harbor so welcoming.

Soldiers who returned there from World War II had never seen a sight more beautiful. They were home, and Bay Harbor welcomed them even if it meant a woman had to give up a cherished job to a returning soldier or a husband saw his wife through eyes with memories she'd never imagine.

Miles away in Kentucky, Bay Harbor had just begun to take shape in the mind of a too thin soldier mustering out at Camp Campbell. Hilton Fields stared at the clothes spread out on his bunk and began jamming them into his duffle bag. A sergeant came by and stopped at his bunk.

"What's the matter, buddy? You're jamming them clothes in there like you're mad at somebody. Aren't you glad to be going home? Jesus Christ, the war's over. You're mustering out, son."

Hilton shoved his trembling hands inside his pockets and looked up with a smile that concealed his thoughts. *I'm not your son, you fat son-of-a bitch. Your hold over me is almost a thing of the past.*

"Just preoccupied, I guess. Thinking of home," he answered.

"We're all thinking the same thing, buddy. Where you from?"

Hilton forced another smile and replied, "No place special, Sarge, just a little town without foxholes."

The sergeant laughed, Hilton saluted, and the guy moved on down the line.

Hilton zipped the duffle bag and sat on the side of his bunk, clutching his hands between his knees. He was thinking of home all right, trying to figure out where that would be. He'd never missed it before, but the war changed all that. He had no desire to go on being a gypsy the rest of his life. Bay Harbor was the only place that came to mind. Perhaps it could offer him a new beginning, the happy event every soldier longed for. Though he knew that for some the return home would be a new look at tragedy, a divorce, a life that no longer fit, he determined to make his fit.

Hilton dismissed the fact that his mother lived in Bay Harbor now, that they'd never gotten along, that he hadn't written her a letter since the war began. He'd written her a letter once, and in return she'd sent him a first grade speller.

His closest friend, Robert Owens, lived in Bay Harbor too, someone else he hadn't written. But he'd make it up to Robert. His mother? She was another matter entirely, but she was old now. And he'd always gotten along with Mr. Richards, his stepfather. Hilton could make it work. He was sure of it. It was a decision that brought him the first happiness he'd known since the war began, and he'd celebrate the only way he knew how. He'd bed the first whore he could find.

Hilton had a way with money and women, but he had yet to really know Bay Harbor. A small town of fewer than 5,000 people, Bay Harbor's impact on its residents was immeasurable. Since his mother and stepfather had moved there, Hilton had visited infrequently and never longer than a day. He had no inkling of the ways Bay Harbor charmed its residents, made them feel special, even when they weren't.

Robert Owens' daughter, twelve year old Anna Lee, thought Bay Harbor made her special, understood she had been living in a memorable time and place. Bay Harbor was all she knew, that and the war.

The war had been the storm that carried people along, gave them purpose, kept them patriotic, loyal, and ready to sacrifice whatever it took to preserve their way of life. Anna Lee cherished all the war had made of them, had already begun to live its memory, wondering how they'd ever get along without it.

Anna Lee's daddy was Bay Harbor's deputy sheriff and a respected member of the community. Her Uncle John was the only pharmacist and the most handsome man in town. And her mother, Estelle, was a sharp-tongued woman who cooked food fit for angels and could have made their robes too if she'd set her mind to it. Anna Lee believed these things gave her status, never realizing she was but a small shell on Bay Harbor's shore.

And now Anna Lee worried that she was betraying her place in Bay Harbor, admitting only to herself that she had loved the war. How could she adjust to life without exciting war movies, the special taste of a piece of candy that was rationed, soldiers in jeeps, Bay Harbor's deep waters bearing ships to war.

Guilt tormented her. What kind of person loved a war! Just one more secret to make her stomach hurt.

Anna Lee wasn't popular within her own age group and gravitated to friendships with older girls. Her favorite was Bay Harbor's beauty, nineteen year old Tyler Rose. She knew Tyler would hate her if she found out how she felt about the war. Her fiancé was in the Navy, and Tyler wrote to him every day.

Tyler seemed to have it all, but local girls took comfort from the fact that, for all her beauty, Tyler's family name would always be Rose, as in Rose Funeral Home. A family business for several generations, it was her constant burden, but one that lightened considerably when World War II brought Tyler her first serious boyfriend.

It was 1943 and while the townspeople drove dull grey and black Chevrolets and Fords that moved like storm clouds on the horizon, Stephen Rayburn, a recent graduate of the Naval Academy in Annapolis, came to town on a spring day crisp and important in his brilliant white uniform. Tall and slender, fine boned and handsome, he cut a fine figure. The people in Bay Harbor were nothing if not impressed, particularly Tyler's mother, Beatrice.

Tyler always told Stephen that she felt his presence even before she saw him in Johnn Owens' drugstore.

"The air felt charged, Stephen. I swear it did." She softened her voice a little, dragged her words more than usual because he'd told her how he enjoyed her liquid vowels. She liked the sound of that. Liquid vowels.

Wars make lots of striking couples, but none more so than Tyler and Stephen. When Tyler linked her arm with Stephen's, her long, deliberate stride matching his, they seemed to own the sidewalk.

The night before Stephen shipped out, he gave Tyler a string of pearls. "They were to be your wedding gift, but I want you to have them now. Even though I'm far away, I'll be able to picture you wearing them." He cupped the pearls in both his palms and kissed them. Twice. When he placed his hands beneath Tyler's shoulder length pageboy and fastened them around her neck, he kissed them again. Tyler knew she was the luckiest girl in the world.

The telegram came in November of 1945. Stuck inside the screen door by an impatient delivery boy, it had been caught in a chill November wind and blown into the garden where Beatrice had sent Tyler to pick some late roses and foliage to brighten the house.

Anna Lee had just started down the sidewalk when she saw Tyler go into the garden. Even as late as November Tyler's olive complexion looked tan, and Anna Lee knew she'd be wearing the pearls Stephen gave her before he left. She never took them off.

Anna Lee's mother said she thought it was bad luck to give some-body a wedding gift early. Anna Lee didn't tell Tyler that. She just watched the pearls grow more luminous with each passing day, the way Tyler said they would.

Anna Lee called, "Hey, Tyler," and stepped through the gate, inhal-ing the earthy smell of neglect and the bitter scent of dying mums. She rubbed her nose on her sleeve and, noticing how pretty Tyler looked, became acutely conscious of her own thin brown hair pulled back with a tacky bow shaped barrette, her bony frame lost inside a blue plaid dress. All her dresses were too big. Her mother made them that way to allow for growth. And though she wore them out before she grew into them, her mother went right on making them too large. Tyler's gray slacks defi-nitely weren't too big.

Anna Lee kicked some dried rose petals and noticed a bit of yellow paper nearly hidden beneath some pine straw mulch. She brushed the dirt off the envelope with her skirt, and said, "Why, it has your name on it, Tyler, but they spelled it with an 'i' instead of a 'y'. I love Tyler with a 'y', but I don't think it's pretty at all with an 'i', do you? It sounds the same and yet it doesn't, knowing the 'y' isn't there. Just like Uncle Johnn having that second 'n' in his name. It keeps it from being so common, don't you think?"

Anna Lee grew quiet when she realized Tyler wasn't listening to her and watched as Tyler placed the basket on the ground as carefully as if it held eggs. Then, still in slow motion, she stretched her hand in the direction of the telegram. She opened it and ran screaming, "Mother! Mother!"

Close on Tyler's heels, Anna Lee could hear Beatrice Rose pleading softly as she took the telegram from Tyler, "Not Stephen, oh God, please don't let it be Stephen." The telegram floated to the floor, and Beatrice gathered the limp and weeping Tyler into her arms. Anna Lee stood there clutching the basket of flowers, trembling so hard her teeth chattered.

Beatrice let out a guttural moan and shouted, "Anna Lee, for the love of God, go home! Tyler's had a terrible shock. Stephen's missing."

Flowers spilled on the floor when Anna Lee dropped the basket and ran out the front door and down the steps. She was closing the gate when Tyler's cousin, T. J., called to her from the porch of the funeral home, "There's a death tour today at four, Anna Lee. Wanna come?"

Anna Lee loved death tours at the funeral home and never missed one if she could help it, but she could think of nothing but the news in the telegram.

"Maybe. I don't know. Stephen's missing." She hadn't stopped running and didn't know if he heard her or not.

Anna Lee's footsteps echoed on the smooth sidewalk as she passed the frame houses of her neighbors, none of them grand, just large, comfortable homes spread beneath sheltering trees. All were painted white, all with front porches that boasted inviting swings, padded wicker furniture, all blurred by her haste. *No one outside to tell.* She glimpsed a gold star framed in the Schneider's window for their son who had been killed in action, and victory gardens where flowers had once bloomed. It wasn't far to her own house, but the sidewalk narrowed and was uneven, far enough to be out of the neighborhood of lovely, gracious homes, far from the crumpled tragedy of a yellow telegram. She ran into the house, much as Tyler had, calling, "Mama! Mama!"

Her mother sat at her Singer sewing machine, the room strong with the odor of machine oil. Estelle pushed the cast iron treadle in a slow, rhythmic motion. Anna Lee knew that had she been angry, her feet would have worked back and forth pressing the treadle to its maximum speed. Taking all this in at a glance, she rushed up and grabbed her mother's arm.

"Anna Lee, you nearly took my breath away!" Estelle pressed her hand to her heart. "Don't do that!"

"But, Mama. . ."

"Don't 'but Mama' me. You about gave me a heart attack."

"Yes, ma'am, but, Mama. . ."

"Anna Lee, just calm down. You're much too excitable these days. God knows how I'm going to handle the change and your puberty at the same time."

"Yes, ma'am." Anna Lee hung her head and started out of the room.

"Anna Lee Owens, get back here! After all that upset, what did you want?"

"It's Stephen. He's missing."

"Stephen?"

"Tyler Rose's Stephen."

"My, God! Is Beatrice Rose having a nervous breakdown?"

"I'm not sure. Tyler's crying."

"Little wonder. As proud as her mother is of that Stephen Rayburn, I'll bet she's crying too. Nothing like realizing your ambitions through your children." Then faster than she could crochet a chain stitch, Estelle added, "Pride goeth before a fall." Estelle wasn't a religious woman but had a preacher's talent for furthering her own purpose with a bit of scripture.

"Not that I'm glad he's missing. I surely hope he's okay. Still, if some people weren't so snooty, it'd be a lot easier to feel sorry for them."

"Tyler's not snooty."

"What would you call her then? She acts like she's the prettiest thing God ever put breath in."

"She's nice to me. I think she's beautiful, like an angel. I've always thought she should teach Sunday school."

"In God's name, why?"

"Because she looks like an angel."

"Angels don't teach Sunday school, Anna Lee. They're musical. They play harps."

"Well, if they know God it seems they could teach Sunday school too."

"Just because you're twelve years old, you don't know everything, Miss." Estelle lifted the fabric from the machine and bit the thread with her teeth.

She frowned at Anna Lee. "What'd you say? You know better than to mumble."

"All those straight pins on the floor. Do you want me to pick them up?"

"No. Now that the war's over, I'll be able to buy all the pins I want. I enjoy throwing the old ones in the garbage, just cause I can."

Anna Lee moved her shoe back and forth over a cluster of pins. "Mama, do you think maybe Stephen got lost on the way home, and they just think he's missing?"

"No I don't. And when it's all over, it'll be a long time before everybody's accounted for. Why, Tyler's daddy hasn't been heard from in God knows how long. Lord help us if Larry's missing too."

"Poor Tyler. She's so young and pretty, and now she has a broken heart."

"You're just a child. You don't know anything about broken hearts."

"Was your heart ever broken?"

"A mother's heart breaks every day."

"I don't mean that way. Remember how sad Miss Amy was when her husband died, before she married Uncle Johnn? Her eyes were always red from crying.

"Well, there's all kinds of heartbreak, same as there's all kinds of love." Estelle glanced at the picture on the back of a Simplicity pattern and then back at the fabric on her sewing machine. "In about a minute you'll be able to hear my heart break if I've cut this pattern wrong."

As she started to leave the room, Anna Lee looked at her mother and hated her a little, hated her for not knowing she was so much more than twelve, that she'd grown old with the burden of protecting her parents, protecting them from finding out she'd learned their secret, that it had become her secret too. Tears blurred her eyes.

The treadle stopped moving and Estelle snapped another thread with her teeth. "Anna Lee, stop staring at me like that. What's the matter with you?"

"Nothing, Mama. I was just thinking."

"Well do your thinking some place else. How can I concentrate with you standing there?"

She squeezed her eyes shut for a moment and then returned to her errand. She had to tell somebody else about the telegram or she'd burst.

Who can I tell? Not T. J. He'd make it his news and run with it like a kite. I know! I'll tell Lola Edwards and her mother. They won't know anything about it at the lighthouse.

CHAPTER
Two

November 1945

Hilton Field's celebration was about to begin. He picked up his duffle bag and walked out into the bright sunlight. He hitched a ride to Hopkinsville where he found a bar and a woman.

Men might not talk about it, but they knew what they looked like the same as women did, and Hilton was never unaware of his striking good looks. Tall and slender with high cheekbones, a strong, wide jaw and straight thick eyebrows that grew close over dark eyes. He was fine. Hadn't enough women told him so? He was fine right down to his most unusual, unforgettable feature—hair the color of sea foam.

He sat on a stool in a saloon filled with drunken soldiers, eager to join them.

The bartender left a group of men at the end of the bar and approached Hilton. "What'll it be, soldier? How does a cold beer sound?"

"No thanks. Jack Daniels and I have been friends a long time now. Splash some over a little ice, and we'll get reacquainted."

A few minutes later the bartender returned with the drink and said, "Here's to you. This should wash away the dust from all those foxholes."

"Then maybe I should order another one right now. Those things were nearly my undoing. Nothing worse than being stuck in a damn foxhole with some guy talking about his sainted mother."

"Hey now, don't go bad mouthing anybody's mother. Not a one of us would be here if we didn't have mothers."

"True." Hilton lifted his glass. "Here's to all those sainted mothers."

"That's more like it, buddy. Enjoy your booze."

Hilton watched the bartender's back as he walked away and then gripped his glass to still his trembling hands, tried to steady his thoughts and prepare himself for a new life, a new existence.

He stared unseeing at the mirror behind the bar, looking inward, sorting his life, trying to find himself. He knew he owed his wealth to Mr. Richards for giving him a tidy sum when he graduated from high school. Hilton never doubted it was a payoff because that diploma brought his schoolteacher mother so much pleasure. He might not know how to spell anything but his name, but he'd worked every damn dollar for a better yield and was a wealthy man before World War II put him on a different path. He hadn't seen clearly since, except to know he wasn't built for combat, that his trembling hands were a constant reminder of what he'd survived.

"Who you looking at in that mirror, soldier?"

"Huh?"

Hilton turned to the woman on the stool beside him, had no idea how long she'd been there. He laid his hand over hers and winked.

"You're a damn sight better looking than the guy in the mirror. How bout we go some place quiet and I'll look at you instead?"

She was a whore, all right. She was off the stool before he could settle his bill.

CHAPTER
Three

Anna Lee ran through the house and out the front door headed toward town and the beach, toward the beauty of the lighthouse. Lola, the lighthouse keeper's daughter as she was known at school, had parents who were striking in their good looks and doted on their fifteen year old daughter. Lola wore store-bought clothes and perfume, but best of all, she called a lighthouse home. It thrilled Anna Lee to touch even the fringes of that existence.

Soon she was skipping down the sidewalk, almost forgetting the news she carried, nearly forgetting the secret that weighed her down. All the times her parents quit talking when she entered a room. She knew why. She understood the menace of unfinished sentences. Anna Lee had to pretend she didn't know Estelle Owens was her stepmother. She pretended because her parents didn't want her to know. They went to such lengths to keep her from finding out that no one in Bay Harbor dared betray their secret, not even Anna Lee.

Anna Lee thought Lola had a fairytale life, one that held none of the problems that tormented her. Lola's daddy, Captain Edwards, was in the Coast Guard and Virginia Edwards was so pretty she didn't look like a mother, but she was. She was Lola's real mother.

Having a stepmother left Anna Lee on the outside looking in, afraid to ask questions about her real mother, a shadowy woman named Grace.

Anna Lee loved the lighthouse, every salt sprayed board and glass prism that Lola took for granted. And she was fascinated by the twin staircases that marked the front entrance to the Edwards' living quarters. Twenty-two steps on either side joined at the top to form a short platform.

Anna Lee's mother told her the steps were originally intended to provide one staircase for men and the other for women. That way, the men couldn't look up the women's dresses when they reached the top of the stairs. Anna Lee didn't know if she was joking or not.

The platform led to a crisp white wrap-around porch, but the real jewel was a crown of glittering, reflecting lenses, the crystal prisms that could dim diamonds, that made it the lighthouse. Across the highway the blue green water of the Gulf of Mexico was bordered by sand so white it might have been sugar. The lighthouse and the beach, each reflecting the other's beauty across time and for all time.

Anna Lee halted her skipping and began running toward the house where salt breezes blew through the windows and whipped white curtains about like ghosts from an ancient shipwreck.

She ran until she had a stitch in her side and slowed down as she cut across the highway near the colored quarters and walked along the beach. The damp sand made tight, squeaky sounds beneath her shoes, and the waves were all froth, thick with crunchy shells. A cold wind blew her rumpled dress between her legs, pressing it tight against her clammy skin. She closed her eyes from time to time and pretended to be Rita Hayworth. She felt beautiful right up to the time she knocked on the Edwards' door. One look at Lola and Anna Lee knew she wasn't beautiful at all.

"You're a mess, Anna Lee. The wind's tangled your hair, and it looks like you slept in that dress." Lola rubbed her hands up and down on her arms. "Come on in and have some cocoa. It'll warm you up."

Anna Lee followed Lola through the front room, breathing in the beauty of the white bead board walls and woven grass rugs. Yellow and green throw pillows, a soft chintz sofa, and wicker furniture made the room bright even on a cloudy day. Magazines were plentiful too, scattered about like fallen leaves, raked into bunches on tabletops and bookcases.

Anna Lee eased gratefully into the high backed wooden seat of the breakfast nook where she could hide her body, all bones and sharp angles, behind the table.

"Don't drink so fast, Anna Lee. Sip, like this." Lola's soft lips pressed gently against the cup, and she swallowed slowly.

"But I'm thirsty. I practically ran here."

"That's no excuse. You never know who might be watching you make a pig of yourself. It's okay here, but you might forget sometime and hate yourself for it. And don't slurp! There's more on the stove."

Sometimes Anna Lee felt like a Girl Scout project Lola had taken on to earn a badge. "Well, you might forget too if you knew what I know."

Lola laughed. "Oh? And what do you know?"

"Tyler Rose's Stephen is missing."

Lola's hand froze with the cup midway to her mouth. "Where'd you hear that? I don't believe it."

"Tyler got a telegram. I saw it."

Lola's eyes brimmed, but Anna Lee noticed that she never lost her composure. She supposed Lola was practicing for the day when someone more important than Anna Lee Owens might be watching, and she'd hate herself for it.

"Poor Tyler. To have your life all planned out and then have it fall apart."

Anna Lee had trouble sitting still. Telling Lola wasn't enough. "Where's your mother?"

"She has a headache. She's lying down."

"She has lots of headaches, doesn't she?" Anna Lee remembered hearing her mother say Virginia Edwards was miserable and wondered if being miserable could account for the headaches.

Lola sighed. "I guess."

Anna Lee mashed a lump of un-dissolved cocoa in her cup, unaware that Lola's mother stood in the doorway.

Virginia Edwards ran her fingers through her blue-black hair and yawned, a pose she affected often. A young man told her once that she looked like Hedy Lamarr, and she'd never forgotten it. "What's this news about a telegram?" she asked in a quiet, sultry voice.

Anna Lee jumped and spilled cocoa on the table. She dabbed it with her napkin and knew she'd dropped another couple of notches in Lola's eyes. Anna Lee longed to say it, to tell Mrs. Edwards about Stephen, but Lola told her instead. Without even looking up, she knew that was Lola's punishment for the spilled cocoa. She vowed to be more careful. She had no intention of losing a friendship that made her welcome at the lighthouse.

In the drugstore one day, Anna Lee overheard Virginia tell Estelle that Lola was approaching sixteen with the seriousness of a thirty year old matron. "I don't know what to do about it, Estelle. I wish she were more like Anna Lee. That child is like a breath of fresh air to our salty old lighthouse."

Estelle, always uncomfortable with a compliment, said, "Well, don't let her be a nuisance."

Anna Lee wasn't sure how to be a breath of fresh air, but she tried very hard to be just that and watched for Virginia's approval. When Anna Lee said that the inside of a fat woman's pocketbook always smelled good, Virginia laughed until tears ran down her face.

"And what does a fat woman's pocketbook smell like?"

"Doublemint chewing gum most often."

"Well, Anna Lee, I'll make a note never to put chewing gum in my purse. Heaven knows, I might get fat."

"Don't encourage her, Mother. She'll just get silly again."

The smile wilted on Virginia's face. She looked at Lola, and said, "Oh, darling, laugh, be silly. Don't squander your youth. You could take a lesson from Anna Lee."

Virginia could have said anything but that. If Tyler was Anna Lee's romantic ideal, Lola was her role model. They had a good teacher/pupil relationship, and it was important that Anna Lee never forget that she was the pupil. Lola pressed her lips together in tight primness. Anna Lee left the table and rinsed her cup and saucer in the sink.

"There's a death tour this afternoon so I'd better go."

Lola made no attempt to conceal her disgust. "I've never understood why you go to those things. It's just plain weird. And childish. I can't believe y'all have never been caught in there."

"It's called the prep room."

"You're joking. The prep room?"

"That's what it's called. I mean, well, the bodies are prepped there. And we don't get caught cause T. J. is so careful. His dad must be out of town or we wouldn't be having one at four." She pulled the barrette from her hair and refastened it.

Virginia spoke up. "I don't believe I know T. J."

"You must have seen him, Mother. He's all over the place. Sometimes I think there must be ten of him. He's a wiry little freckle faced kid with squinty eyes." Virginia looked at Anna Lee. "Maybe I've seen him. Where's his mother during all this?"

"She's a nurse and never gets home from work before 5:30, but we don't have death tours during the day that often. Nighttime is best, especially when it's storming." She thought of how flashes of lighting illuminated the grisly equipment and added a touch of brimstone to the throat-gagging smell. "T. J. charges more for the tours when it's storming."

Virginia and Lola seemed quite speechless with all this information, but when Anna Lee got to the door Lola called, "All those dead bodies. Doesn't it smell awful in there?"

"It sure doesn't smell like the inside of a fat woman's purse." As she closed the door she could hear Virginia starting to laugh again.

CHAPTER
Four

Friday, 4 p.m.

The funeral home had the abandoned look common to a death tour. The grounds were deserted. Even the leaves hung motionless on the trees, but Anna Lee knew there'd be a crowd of boys and a few girls hidden in the hedges.

She saw some movement and slipped behind a hedge herself. She heard one of the boys say, "Didn't I tell you Anna Lee would be here? She never misses a death tour."

Anna Lee smiled, pleased with the respect she'd earned by her near perfect attendance, her lack of fear.

When T. J. whistled from the front door, they filed out like ants, up the steps and across the porch without a word. As soon as they were all inside, T. J. held his hand up to stop them. "Now remember," he said in an undertone, "any noise, a scream or anything louder than a whisper, and I'll make you drink embalming fluid. Is there anybody that thinks I couldn't do it?" Their belief was evident in their silence.

"Let me go in first," T. J. said. "A body exploded in here the other day, and I want to be sure they've cleaned it up."

Somebody whispered, *"Exploded?"*

A few minutes later, T. J. emerged from the prep room and said softly, "It's clean." He held the door open, and let them inhale the forbidding odor of embalming fluid and formaldehyde before he motioned them inside. When the door was closed the metal click of the key turning in the lock echoed throughout the dark room. The air was heavy and close.

T. J. drew a deep, audible breath. "That's death we're smelling," he said quietly. There's nothing else like it."

"Exploded?" someone repeated.

"Tissue gas," T. J. replied with authority. "It's evil stuff. Nobody knows where it comes from, not even my dad. If it gets in a body it'll explode. Personally, I think it's ghost gas."

T. J. got out a flashlight so he could see to turn on a small lamp in the far corner. The dim light revealed fans like tall trees filling two corners of the room. A metal table on wheels and a smaller instrument table cast cold reflections. A rubber apron of dull black hung from a wooden coat rack.

Eyes were wide and breathing labored. The death tour had begun.

"Everybody hold hands now," T. J. instructed. "I don't want y'all knocking things over."

Feet scuffled and there was the sound of flesh striking flesh. Whispered "no, wait, stop" hung moist on the air.

T. J. hissed, "I didn't tell you to dance. Grab a hand. NOW! I ain't got all day." He waited a minute and whispered, "Come over here and place your dimes on the embalming table."

Anna Lee led the way, and the others followed.

"While you're there, feel how cold that table is."

T. J. was a master showman. He lowered his whisper even deeper. "That's the chill every dead body leaves behind. Be careful you get your dimes on the table and not in the grooves on the side. The blood and fluid drains out of the body into them grooves. It might still be wet, and I don't want no wet dimes."

Most often the boys let go of their dimes palm down on the table. The girls' dimes made a clanging sound when they dropped them.

"T. J.," one of the boys asked, "where do the body fluids go, after they run down the grooves?"

"Into the sewer, stupid. Where do you think?"

They stepped back and waited for T. J.'s next move.

"I wish I could get y'all in here sometime when a body's here. Ever hear a dead man talk?" At the sound of indrawn breath he went on. "You know our maid?"

Anna Lee knew that was her cue. "The one with the bulging eyes?"

"Yeah, that's the one. Pansy. Her eyes got that way cause she came in this room. She was new and didn't know this was the prep room. About the time she walked in the door, the man on the table let out a loud groan."

"No!" someone whispered.

"Don't doubt me," T. J. threatened. "It happens all the time. The dead man groaned, and she saw my dad jab this trocar," T. J. walked to the instrument table and picked up a metal pipe with a sharp blade on the end, "into the man's stomach to get out the excess fluid. Her eyes wasn't never the same again. My dad said he thought they'd pop right out of her head."

A small girl's voice quavered. "I've seen her."

"Hellfire and brimstone!" T. J. positioned the trocar on the instrument tray.

Somebody whispered. "He knows more curse words than any boy in school."

"SHH!" T. J. turned off the lamp. No one moved; few dared breathe. Someone was walking up the outside steps. "My mom must be home early. You got your dime's worth anyhow."

T. J. unlocked the door and they ran on tiptoe shoving and pushing to get out of the room and through the front door as quietly as they'd come. Nobody would drink embalming fluid that day. Children scattered in all directions before Mary got up the stairs and inside her front door.

T. J. followed Anna Lee out and they sat on the steps to the Rose's upstairs apartment. He handed her a dime.

"That body didn't really explode, did it?"

"Nah. It's just noisy gas that comes out, but I wanted to give them their money's worth."

"I like stormy nights best."

"Me too. And not just cause I charge more."

"You don't think I'm scared in there, do you?"

"I know you ain't. Why do you think I always give your dime back?"

"I don't come for the same reason the others do. I come because death fascinates me."

"Me too."

"T. J."

"Yeah?"

"You hear about Stephen?"

"Aunt Beatrice told me. I hope he ain't dead though. Just cause we're in the business, I don't like it when people die."

"Me either." She looked at the freckles that lay across his nose like a dusting of cinnamon. They gave him an air of innocence he didn't deserve.

His mother called his name, and they hooked pinky fingers before he turned and ran upstairs.

Death is never welcome, but in small towns, especially in the South, the funeral home has always held an exalted position among a community's most respected, stately and well maintained houses. Bay Harbor was no exception. Forget the grief, loss and even betrayal brought there by generations of mourning families. Rose Funeral Home was a towering Victorian landmark in a community given primarily to modest frame and brick homes of only one floor.

Broad porches, white as clouds, embraced the funeral home on three sides, making all who entered feel as though they had already arrived in heaven. It was a comforting balm to the bereaved and a hope for the hopeless.

Long before the name took on special meaning associated with a grim but necessary occupation, it had been the home place of the Rose family.

It had always been painted some shade of blue, and the house once sat square in the middle of twenty wooded acres. Over time and hard times, much of the land had either been sold or divided into home sites for offspring. Less than an acre remained around the undertaking establishment, but every inch was a lush carpet of green grass, fragrant juniper hedges, camellias, bridal wreath, purple iris and a bower of ivy and seasonal sweet peas.

The current living occupants had no intention of falling on hard times. To economize they converted part of the upstairs into their living quarters, its only entry an outside stairway toward the back of the house.

When business was slow T. J.'s dad, Foster Rose, helped out in Johnn Owens' drugstore. Some people felt uneasy seeing Foster there, but Dr. Owens did all the mixing and pill counting. Foster bagged things and talked to people while they waited.

Foster was as nice to people in the drugstore as when they had business in his own establishment. He was a large pleasant-looking man with a head of thick wavy hair and a naturally cheerful disposition. It was a good thing too. There wasn't a cheerful bone in his wife's body. Long hours and hard work had stripped Mary of her beauty and left her dour and pinched, looking more like an undertaker than her husband.

Mary was the only nurse in the office of Dr. Samuel Mason, and Dr. Mason himself said a smile was a stranger on Mary's face. He couldn't have cared less if she smiled, though. She was a competent nurse, the only one in town who could give a baby a shot without making it cry. Young mothers were especially fond of her, and Dr. Mason knew it.

Working as hard as Mary and Foster did left them little time for their eleven-year old son. Foster could drain the blood out of a dead man and an hour later be comforting his family of wailing relatives. Equally competent, Mary could plunge an enema tube into the richest, fattest man in town without blinking an eye. Neither would he. Babies and fat men loved her.

But T. J. stumped them both. He was never still long enough for his parents to really understand him. He was always moving, bent forward from the waist, rushing some place. They were never quite sure where. At night sometimes they'd tiptoe into his room and watch him sleeping. Even then he looked as though he might jump up and run out the door at any moment. Sometimes he did after he was sure his parents were asleep.

Everybody in town knew how seriously the Roses took their business. Foster and Mary expected their rowdy youngster to regard their establishment as more of a shrine than a home. The funeral home belonged to Bay Harbor, to the dead, to the ages. The Roses were only caretakers.

T. J. was forbidden to use the front entrance or to play on the pristine porches. "Death deserves dignity," his father would intone in his best funeral voice. "We owe the dead that much. Sometimes it's the only dignity a body's ever had."

T. J. wasn't terribly bothered by all the rules. There were enough hours in the day when his parents weren't around for him to do pretty much as he liked, and nobody ever told on him. It didn't seem right that the Roses should have more concern for the dead than the living.

February 1946

The New Year came around, and people continued to feel they were walking under a cloud, fighting against stupor. What happened to the euphoria they expected from a war that had ended? Where were the men who still hadn't returned? They had rolled bandages, saved scrap metal, purchased war bonds, watched ships sail to war from their harbor, made sacrifices, and now idle hands left them uneasy.

Guilt weighed on them for they couldn't forget the dead whose hands were idled forever. The people in Bay Harbor had as much respect for the dead as the next person, and never more so than during World War II, but they longed for some return to normalcy. If there was a family in town that hadn't lost a son or brother or husband, they knew someone who had. Perhaps normalcy had died, too.

Emily Richards was all too aware of Bay Harbor's losses, had endured the war without word of her son and worried he might one day be counted among Bay Harbor's dead. Her letters to Hilton had gone unanswered but not returned. Those unreturned letters were her only ray of hope. She'd buried her second husband since the war began, and she prayed

God she wouldn't have to bury a son as well. She was old, had lived her life. God should take her, not Hilton.

Having been brought up never to air dirty linen, Emily had always found it difficult to form close friendships, but she had to talk to someone and confided in her servant girl, Annie.

She followed the young woman to the kitchen and pulled a chair next to the window facing the garden.

"I have so much, Annie. I know I've been blessed, but I'd trade it all if I could have been closer to Hilton. I was so intent on shaping him when I should have just been loving him instead."

"We can only do what we can do, Miz Richards."

"I tried, oh believe me, Annie, I wanted to show him how much I cared, but I seemed incapable. Incapable. And now it's too late."

"It's never too late to let somebody know you love them."

Emily gave a harsh laugh. "Annie, don't you understand? I still don't know how."

Hilton heard thunder when he left the bus station. He gazed at the darkening sky, smiled and prayed.

God in heaven, tell me I'm not making a mistake. Mother is older, ripe for mellowing. Surely Bay Harbor is big enough for one old woman and her maverick son.

He made his way from the bus station to the main street. People walked past him, some nodding, others saying hello, but no one recognized him. He hadn't been to Bay Harbor in years, and he'd never known a great many people in the first place. He figured Robert would be at the police station, but he made no move to go there.

He could feel his hands trembling inside his pockets. He needed to rest. He wanted nothing more than to see Robert, to make things right with him, to change his life, but it could wait a bit longer.

He chuckled to himself thinking of how they played practical jokes on each other when they were boys. Well, he'd have the last laugh. He'd play a joke on Robert he'd never forget, but not now. If he got some rest first maybe he could still his trembling hands. Maybe it would be best if he avoided his mother, take the next bus out and lay low for a while, not answering to anybody.

Hilton heard another rumble of thunder and watched lightning bleed across the sky. He turned up the collar of his trench coat and walked a few blocks to Johnn Owens' drugstore. He stepped just inside the door. No fetid smell of raw blood and dank foxholes here. He took a deep breath and inhaled the fragrance of malted milks, ladies' dusting powder and medicine; nothing to make his hands tremble, but he found the familiarity disturbing. His whole future had changed while here life went on as though there'd never been a war. He saw Doc Owens and then the guy who ran the funeral home still there helping out in his spare time he supposed. Hilton couldn't place his name but felt the urge to punch him out just for being there. A man in the business of death passing out medicine to sustain life. Life and death in one bottle. For a frightening moment Hilton feared he might cry but turned on his heel instead and went out the door, never noticing the lovely Virginia Edwards whose knees grew weak at the sight of him, memory and lust causing her to clutch the glass display case to steady herself.

CHAPTER
Five

Early March 1946

Tyler Rose sat up in the coffin and screamed. Foster and Mary heard screams in their upstairs apartment. Beatrice heard them from her front porch. They all came running. Footsteps pounding on the wooden floor.

When Beatrice saw Tyler, her unwashed hair clinging to her head, the pallor of her skin as light as the quilted lining of the casket, she began screaming too. With that, Tyler grew silent, closed her eyes and let her head fall back on the pillow.

Mary tried to shush her sister-in-law. "Beatrice, control yourself. What'll the neighbors think? Remember the business we're in for heaven's sake."

Foster placed his palm on Tyler's forehead, checked her pulse, turned and slapped Beatrice to shut her up. It was something he'd longed to do for years. He'd told Mary on more than one occasion that Beatrice might look solid and practical, but in reality she was oftentimes a fool.

"Oh, dear Lord, dear Lord," Beatrice cried," she's taken something! Sweet Jesus, she's dying! Mary! Have you left pills around here? She must have gotten into some dope."

"Lord in heaven, Beatrice! Are you so stupid that you think I bring medicine home? I have a child too, you know. I'm sick and tired of you blaming me for things, looking down your nose at me . . ."

"Y'all cut it out now. Both of you." Foster lifted Tyler from the casket, but her knees gave way, and Foster scooped her into his arms and started out of the showroom. Before he reached the door Mary had begun smoothing the satin lining.

"Foster, we won't say a word about this."

"Of course not. It's nobody's business."

Beatrice was whimpering, the red bloom of Foster's hand still on her face. "Thank you, Mary. I promise you this won't happen again. It's just that we've had so much . . ."

"I know, and it won't go any farther than this room. As far as Foster and I are concerned, it never happened. This is still a new casket." She moved her hand over the polished wood. "Never been used. We can still get full price for it."

Beatrice blinked and Tyler came to laughing. Foster was afraid he might have to slap her too, but there'd be no pleasure in it. "Let it go, Mary. Forget about money for once. This is family." He continued across the hall to the receiving room and eased Tyler onto a sofa. "Just rest here, darlin'. If we go upstairs all the neighbors will be a gawking at you."

"I'm sorry, Uncle Foster. I don't remember coming here. I was sitting on the front porch thinking of Stephen, wanting to die."

"You feel that way now, darlin', but there'll be better times. I guess I've seen about as much grief as anybody, but you're young, and time's a balm for the heart. It really is. I don't mean you'll quit loving Stephen, but it won't be the burden it is today. He'll always be part of your life, but you'll add other loves, and Stephen will blend and become part of them too."

"It's just getting there, Uncle Foster. Getting through this time."

"I know. Dying is part of the contract we have for living, but some of us get shortchanged." Foster paused. "You should quit imagining, rememberin'. There's only sorrow in it now. And you have enough just wonderin' what's happened to your dad. Your mother has her own grief, you know."

"Oh, I know I'm being selfish, thinking of myself. I do worry about Daddy, but he got to live. He and Mother had a life for awhile."

Foster smiled. "Why do young people think it's easier to give up someone who's shared your every breath for years than someone you've only begun to know?"

"Maybe because of the way they treat each other."

Foster winced. "I know, hon. They don't make a very good example of romantic love. I admit people take each other for granted sometimes. We think life's gone go on the way it always has. Your mother has taken a curve ball she hadn't expected."

"You think I'm awful, don't you?"

"No, darlin', I think you're unhappy, but you've got to fight it. None of us can do it for you. You're young and beautiful." He smiled. "But it wouldn't hurt if you quit sitting on the front porch all the time, if you started washing your hair and trying to take care of yourself again. I've always thought you were one of the prettiest girls I've ever known. I want to see that pretty girl again, see her smile." He didn't tell her there was something about her that nearly frightened him, something in her slender, almost boyish figure that betrayed itself in the definition of her jutting breasts, in her full lips and narrow green eyes that never appeared friendly.

"I'll try. I really will."

Like just about everyone else in Bay Harbor, Beatrice thought *Gone With the Wind* was the best book ever written. What she failed to realize was that it wasn't an advice manual. Scarlett's mother sent her to Atlanta to recover from her grief, but since Beatrice had no relatives in Atlanta, she got the bright idea of taking Tyler to visit a widowed cousin in Charleston. Such a wonderful book. Why hadn't she thought of it sooner! She knew the change would do Tyler good, would do them both good.

Envisioning herself as Scarlett's beloved mother, Beatrice completely forgot Charleston's history, that the Civil War began at Fort Sumter, that The Citadel was there. Completely forgot, she'd say later.

They drove to Charleston, a long two day trip, and not once did Tyler offer to help her mother drive. Fighting sleep, Beatrice couldn't help but think how fortunate it was for Scarlett's mother that she hadn't been the one who had to take her to Atlanta. Still, it would be worth the exhaustion if it helped Tyler.

When they drove up, dusty and tired, cousin Sara Louise came running down the front steps of her two-story brick home, arms open wide, declaring, "Oh, Beatrice Rose, you are a sight for sore eyes. And look at you, Tyler!" She kissed her on the cheek. "Come on in the house out of this March wind and let's have some hot tea. You must be starved, and supper is on the stove."

The change did seem to agree with Tyler. She slept late and drank cup after cup of strong coffee as she ate low country grits and shrimp Sara Louise served for breakfast each morning.

Nearly giddy with relief, one day Beatrice suggested they go into town and look at some of the lovely old homes and take a peek at Charleston's walled gardens. "There's not much of a chill in the air today. Don't you think that would be fun?"

"No, I don't," Tyler began before she remembered the promise she'd made her Uncle. They left just after lunch. It was a pleasant walk. Moss laden trees grew over the sidewalks where they looked at beautiful old homes of stuccoed brick.

Beatrice was peeking through the gate of a walled garden when the cadets turned a corner and Tyler saw them, by twos and threes, by groups and single. The uniformed cadets coming toward them were Tyler's undoing. She watched them as they began walking in a circle, faster and faster. Her knees buckled and she swayed, one of the young men dashing forward to break her fall and ease her to a bit of grass.

For once Beatrice kept her composure and knelt beside her unconscious daughter. She thanked the young man and told him they'd be okay. The cadets continued on, and she spoke to the silence of a warm day, "They didn't wear navy whites. They weren't naval officers." But as cousin Sara Louise would point out to her later, they were military, part and parcel of the same brotherhood.

Unable to cope with the hysterical young woman who returned to her home, Sara Louise called a doctor who kept Tyler sedated until she calmed down enough for Beatrice to risk the trip back to Bay Harbor. And while they waited, home was changing.

In mid March of 1946 Larry Rose came home with a metal plate in his head and the holes in his gut patched. It was dusk when he walked from the bus station, taking all the back roads and shortcuts to avoid seeing anyone he knew.

Beatrice and Tyler probably think I'm dead. He knew his dog tags and most of his clothes had been blown off at Omaha Beach. He was taken to a hospital in England. For months nobody knew who he was, not even Larry.

After what he'd been through he didn't have to answer to anybody if he didn't feel like it. God knew he was in Bay Harbor right now standing alone on the front porch of his house, not a light on any place. He stood looking around, grateful that the dusk of a fading day shielded him from prying eyes.

The house had the look of abandonment, as though no one lived there any more. The way he'd looked for a time. The white paint had a grayish cast, and leaves from the magnolia tree littered the front porch. Beatrice's prized roses needed pruning and mulching. Most telling perhaps were the rocking chairs tilted forward against the wall, a sign of disuse. For how long? Well, he hadn't told them he was coming. He hadn't written. Maybe Beatrice had left him.

He pulled the screen door open and hesitated. The oval glass in the heavy oak door looked frosted against the white privacy curtains. It tried to evoke a memory he couldn't capture.

He stood for some minutes before he tested the feel of the metal doorknob in his palm. He took a deep breath and felt it turn beneath his hand. The house wasn't locked so they must be coming back. Relieved the lights weren't on, he stood in the hollowness of the darkened hall, inhaling the stale fragrance of his former life. He dreaded turning on the lights in the same way he dreaded seeing Beatrice. The curtain would be raised and he would be expected to resume the life of a stranger. How could they ever understand? How could he begin to explain? For the first time there was a tiny sliver of doubt that God's saving his life on Omaha Beach had been a blessing after all.

His eyes grew accustomed to the dark, and the streetlight on the corner gave just enough illumination for him to make his way to the living room. The house was close and hot so he raised the side windows facing the street and the three facing the front porch. He could see the upstairs lights on at his brother's across the street.

Larry knew he should go over and let them know he was home, ask where Beatrice and Tyler were, but he couldn't bring himself to do it. Foster was in the business of death, the family business for three generations now, and Larry was weary of death. He'd dwelt there too long.

He stretched out on the living room sofa, surprised by the comfort its familiarity brought him. So this is home, he thought. And that was his last thought until the noise of the ice truck woke him. He looked at his watch, stunned that he'd slept so late. Nearly eleven o'clock! Morning shone through the windows as though he'd never been away. God had turned on the lights when he couldn't. Well, he had been away, but he was back, and he'd have to face the music. God hadn't saved him to waste his life. It had to count for something now.

He hadn't undressed the night before, and his mouth tasted worse than dirty socks, but like a dog waking from a long illness, he went from room to room, learning things again.

The doctors told him there might be some memory loss, so he wanted to test the waters. The living room where he'd slept on the couch didn't look any different. But maybe those were new covers Beatrice had put on the furniture. The broad blue and burgundy stripes looked too bright and cheerful in the morning sunshine.

The dining room had the same dark walnut furniture they'd inherited from his mother. Turning back he forced himself to look at the bedrooms. Tyler's room was much the same, crisp yellow and white, clean and fresh as a young virgin. He walked with heavy steps to the door of the room that, until the war, had been his and Beatrice's. He stared at the four-poster bed and dreaded sharing it with his wife again. Maybe she wouldn't care if he never touched her; something inside him thought she'd probably prefer it that way. He hoped so. How could he touch Beatrice with the memory of Heather still on his hands?

It'd been years since he'd experienced real passion with Beatrice, with anyone but Heather. But Heather was England, the war. She belonged to another time, another place. He was home now. He fought to forget her, all the while remembering.

What happened to people? He'd grown accustomed to their ways, his and Beatrice's. You didn't question. In many ways you didn't think. You just acted, moving from one habit to another. And then he met Heather and understood love for the first time in his life.

He gripped the doorframe so hard his hands ached. He turned away without stepping a foot inside and sought the safety of the kitchen.

He was sure the linoleum on the floor wasn't new. He remembered the worn spots so well. The old Kelvinator refrigerator purred; the cabinets might have been freshly painted. They gleamed white against the red counter tops and crisp white curtains.

Everywhere he looked he could see red. The color of blood. It wasn't his favorite color, and it surrounded him. But then he looked at the red-checkered tablecloth on the kitchen table and realized he wanted a cup of coffee.

Eating and drinking had become a necessity for living, nothing more than habit. He couldn't recall when he'd really wanted anything, but right then he wanted the smell of coffee to fill the kitchen. When he turned on the tap, it choked and spit with disuse. Just like me, he thought.

He found the old dented percolator in the cabinet and remembered exactly how to make a pot of coffee. Over the course of two hours, he drank the entire pot, sitting there at the table sliding his hand rhythmically across the cloth as one might comfort a loved one. He was washing out the pot when he heard the front door slam.

He could hear Tyler trying to calm her mother as Beatrice called in a frightened voice, "Is somebody here? Foster, is that you? Mary? Foster? T. J.?"

How many names would the stupid woman call as she stood there in the safety of the front hall? He'd have to face her now. She might give out of names soon. Oh why was he feeling so hateful? Why couldn't she mean as much as a cup of coffee?

He left the pot in the sink, wiped his hands back and forth on his pants and turned to face a battle more dreaded than Normandy.

Beatrice stood beside a piece of luggage, her black sharkskin dress accenting the weight she'd added while he was away. Larry drew a deep breath and stepped into the hall. Beatrice fainted dead away when she saw him.

Not for the first time, Larry thought that for a healthy, strapping woman, she sure did faint a lot. They'd been married only a few weeks when she grew faint in the bathroom one afternoon and laid down on the bathmat she'd tossed over the back steps that morning to dry in the sun. Eyes shut tight, she took deep breaths, she told him later. When she felt less dizzy, she opened her eyes and saw a snake close by her nose. A frog was a few inches away. She'd brought them inside in the bathmat! She hadn't needed smelling salts that time.

Who am I, he wondered, the snake or the frog?

Then he noticed Tyler, tears running down her face, saw how thin she was. He grabbed her to him for a brief hug before he knelt to revive his wife.

He brushed the back of his hand over his eyes and then carried Beatrice to the living room and propped her up on the sofa. Tyler went for the smelling salts, and they brought her around. Larry was kneeling beside her when she opened her eyes. Her eyes rolled back, and for a moment he thought she was going to faint again.

"I'm sorry, darling. This isn't much of a welcome home. I just never expected you to be here."

"Where else would I go?"

"That isn't what I meant, Larry."

"Just forget it. I'm home now. It's over."

Later Beatrice told Larry that for all the shock of it, she was glad things happened the way they did. The visit to Charleston had been a disaster, an utter disaster, but Larry's returning the way he did seemed to unlock something in Tyler. She quit spending so much time on the porch and started piecing her life back together.

They all did, but for Beatrice and Larry the pieces made a crazy quilt pattern.

One morning, less than a week later, just as Beatrice was pouring her first cup of coffee, Larry told her he didn't want to practice law any more. Hot coffee spilled out of the cup and onto the red checked tablecloth. Beatrice slammed the coffeepot down and dropped into a chair.

"I want to work with Foster at the funeral home."

"You what?"

"I want to use some of our nest egg to expand the business by selling tombstones, special tombstones with life scenes I'll create. They'll depict how people lived, not how they died. I've already made arrangements with Foster. They've opened a new section of the old cemetery. The time is right."

"That's the most ridiculous thing I've ever heard of, Larry. You're a lawyer, not a stone cutter."

"I don't intend to carve the stone, Beatrice. I'll do the drawings, make a template and then advise the stone cutter on what I want. Foster and I have it all worked out."

"Please tell me you're joking."

"It's no joke, Bea." He lowered his head and pushed his hair back with his right hand, a weary gesture. "I wish I could explain it. I just feel I have to be in the business of death, to suffer for being spared, to have a closer connection with God." It seemed so logical to him. He'd thought of little else since he got home. He knew it would be difficult with the memories he carried of wounded and dying men on Omaha Beach, but he supposed that was part of the bargain. He owed God that.

Beatrice fainted dead away before he finished talking. Fortunately she didn't fall off the chair so he didn't have to pick her up. He folded a cold cloth and laid it across her head, just the way Heather had done for him. He touched his forehead where the swelling had been.

Beatrice's head slumped forward, and Larry propped her against the table and went for the smelling salts. She could stay out longer than Frank Sinatra's vocal chords could hold a note.

The smelling salts worked every time. She opened her eyes and said, "Oh, Larry honey, don't cry. I'll be okay." She patted his hand, and he noticed how fat her fingers were, how they squeezed her wedding band. Larry left the room. He hadn't realized he was crying.

While stationed in England, he'd gone with a buddy who wanted to take his sweetheart some food. God only knew where he'd gotten it, the tinned ham worth a king's ransom in England at the time, some chocolate, and a small amount of real coffee. Larry was pretty sure the coffee had been stolen.

The apartment building was dark with low ceilings. When his buddy knocked on a door with scaling paint, a young woman answered, and he followed her into her apartment. Larry, taller by several inches, forgot to duck and hit his head on the doorjamb. He staggered backward just as another young woman came up the stairs. He'd fallen against her and nearly knocked her over. She dropped her parcels and bent to pick them up. Apologizing, he knelt beside her to help. When he glimpsed her face, he nearly lost his breath.

She was stunning. Her long brown hair was wavy, and smelled clean and soapy. She had large silver gray eyes and a dainty nose. She laughed when she saw he'd quit picking up her packages and was staring at her. They stood at the same time, and nearly collided again. She was tall and slender. Like Tyler, he thought. He turned to look for his buddy and saw the door was closed.

The woman laughed again. "I'm Heather. You'd better come with me so I can tend to that bump on your head. But duck this time."

He'd never expected to fall in love. Hadn't planned on any of it. But he and Heather were both scared and lonely. She'd known by then her husband wasn't coming back.

He came to love the small, cramped kitchen where they prepared meals together. She used an old tea cart for a table, wheeling it up to a sofa where their shoulders touched as they ate. There was a dresser, a small chest and a double bed in the bedroom. On his second visit he had asked to use the loo. The door was uneven and stuck when he tried to close it. He had to shove hard to open it again, just as Heather approached, bringing him a clean towel. He'd knocked her backward onto the bed.

When she made no move to get up, he lowered his body onto hers. It felt so innocent, so right. He'd never dreamed someone that lovely could also love him. Maybe she wouldn't have if they hadn't been at war. But they were, and Heather was his only escape. He didn't feel much guilt at the time. Just tried to go on living, to find some pleasure, some comfort before he was blown to bits like so many of his friends had been.

Beatrice and Tyler might not have existed.

CHAPTER
Six

Estelle pressed her stomach against the wash basin and reached into the medicine cabinet for the Ipana toothpaste. She looked at the tube for a long time before she squeezed some onto her toothbrush. She was preoccupied with thoughts of her accomplishments as a seamstress. She took great pride in that skill. She made her own housedresses and all of Anna Lee's clothes, even her coats. The year Anna Lee had a part in the Nutcracker Christmas program at school, Estelle made all the costumes, complete with matching umbrellas. They were only crepe paper, but it was a lot of work, and the schoolteachers regarded her with new respect when they saw them.

Estelle thrived on the praise her work brought her, but sewing from necessity was a chore. Unable to replace the worn living room sofa, she'd already made a slipcover. But even that wouldn't be enough with money so tight. Robert had begun hinting she might have to find a job. Lots of women had taken jobs during the war, but the war was over, and they'd gone back home where they belonged. Estelle's face burned with humiliation at the thought of having to find a job. She was afraid her own war was just beginning.

But what really rankled her was that her sister-in-law was like the lady in the poem who could sit on a cushion and sew a fine seam. Amy didn't have to demean herself by working, not with Johnn Owens supporting her, not with the money she'd inherited from her first husband. No, there were no money problems there.

Estelle loved Robert. At least she thought she did. He was honest and reliable, still nice looking. He wasn't a large man, but muscular and neat. His black hair, smoothed with Brilliantine, was receding a bit, but his face was smooth and unlined. She knew his body as well as her own, and their lovemaking lacked the passion of youth. After a time, how could you be sure you were in love? How could you recognize love after years of habit and compromise? Her heartbeat didn't quicken; there was no excitement. They just belonged.

Estelle spit white foam into the basin and grabbed the cool, hard sides to steady herself. Robert was waiting in bed for them to talk. Well, he'd better keep his hands to himself if he wanted to talk. She was in no mood tonight.

She heard his soft laughter, and it enraged her. Grabbing a handkerchief, she pulled the chain that turned off the hanging light bulb, took a deep breath, and hurried to the bedroom. "What are you laughing about?" she snapped and dropped into bed with unaccustomed heaviness. "I, for one, don't find anything funny about this talk you're planning. If you think it's so funny, please tell me. I could use a good laugh."

"Nah, I don't think it's funny. I was just thinkin' of something one of the guys said down at the station today."

"I can never get over how you can call that metal outhouse a police station."

"Well, I owe my living to that metal outhouse, as you call it."

"That could be a point of disagreement right there. If I'm not mistaken, you're about to tell me I have to get a job. You call that a living? Maybe you should call it almost a living. Half a living. Half-assed living, if you ask me."

Robert's voice was hard, unfriendly. "I cain't recall asking you. Just cause you got to help out for a little while don't give you the right to be so damned hateful. I know you don't want to go to work, Estelle. God knows, I sure as hell hate to ask you, but I don't know any other way. Unless you want to take in washing and ironing."

"Very funny. You're a real comedian tonight, aren't you?"

"I ain't trying to be funny, Estelle. This is serious. We got to pay our bills. You was the one that wanted to buy this house so damn bad. You didn't want to rent. You wanted to own your own house, paint the rooms any color you wanted to. Them was your exact words. Well, if you want to paint them, you gone have to help buy the paint."

"It was just a figure of speech, Robert."

"A what? I swear to God, you sound more like Amy every damn day."

"I'm not trying to sound like Amy. I just meant I wanted the house to be ours, not on loan to us. Johnn and Amy own their house. Every time I turned around, it seemed like Skip Wallace was at the door playing land-lord with his hand out and always craning his neck around, looking to see if we were keeping the place to his satisfaction. It got so I was scared to hang a picture."

"Well, you can do anything you want to now, but you're gone have to pay the price for doing it. There's not enough money coming in, and you know it. Just cause you want to own things like Johnn and Amy do, don't forget you didn't come into any inheritance the way Amy did."

"No, Robert, I don't have an inheritance from a dead husband. If I'm not mistaken you're still among the living."

"Yeah, and if I wasn't, there wouldn't be much inheritance, I tell you. And there ain't nobody around that's gone die and leave us well fixed. I wish there was, but there's not." He sighed and spoke softly, almost to himself. "God, what'd it be like to inherit money, to just glide onto easy street."

"I haven't seen easy street yet and bet we never will." She touched the handkerchief to the corners of her eyes.

"No, we won't, that's for damn sure. It's up to us, Estelle. We got to make our own way."

"But I think we can, Robert. We just have to plan. You love to hunt, and we can eat mostly game. I can plant a bigger garden out back and . . ."

"You're not making good sense, woman! How am I gone buy the shells and stuff I need for hunting? It's more than food, and you know it. For God's sake, Estelle, I'm not happy about this. It's not some punishment I thought up. But marriage is a partnership, and I need you to hold up your end of the bargain."

"Are you implying that I haven't been? Who cleans the house, does the washing—in the back yard, I might add—the ironing, makes nearly every stitch Anna Lee and I wear, cooks the meals. Need I go on?"

"I'm not implying nothing. You're a good wife. A good mother to Anna Lee. I don't need to tell you that. But we're in this for better or worse, and right now it's worse."

Estelle was fighting back tears when she spoke. "I don't know what I can do. I've never been anything but a telephone operator, and somebody'll have to die before Bay Harbor ever needs another one."

"You sew awful good, Estelle, but I cain't see you taking in work. I was thinking maybe you'd like to work for Johnn, in the drugstore."

At that Estelle burst into tears. "Work for Johnn? How could you? I can't believe you even thought that, much less said it. Why, can you imagine me having to wait on the heiress, Amy Owens? Being like a servant?" She slapped her pillow hard and turned her back to him. "Oh, Robert, I thought you loved me more than that. You haven't said anything to Johnn about it, have you? Tell me you haven't said anything to Johnn. He'd tell Amy. I know he would."

"Do you honestly think I'd say anything to Johnn before I talked it over with you?" The lie went down slick as a raw oyster. "I was just thinking it'd look better for you, that's all. I mean, we do still own a little bit of interest in the drugstore."

"We might own a doorknob."

"Well, nobody else has to know we took out nearly all our investment to buy this house. In the eye of the law, we're still part owners. You see, hon, this way, you wouldn't be just some sales clerk. You'd be an investor looking out for your business. More like a store manager. It'd sure take a burden off Johnn."

Estelle sat up in bed and blew her nose. "Why, Robert, I'm surprised at you. You really have thought this out. And you know, that might be the easiest way out of this. I wouldn't really be working *for* Johnn. I'd be sort of my own boss."

"That's what I was thinking, Stelle."

"You just amaze me sometimes, Robert. You really are a smart man. John may be the one with an education, but he isn't the only Owens with brains."

Robert snorted. "That's for damn sure." He didn't say a word about it having been John's idea.

"Maybe I could make myself up some uniforms. Something to look professional, like John does in his white coat."

"I'm sure John would like that. And I know he'll appreciate the help. You and John are going to make a fine team."

Estelle stiffened. "How can you be so sure if you haven't talked to him yet?"

"Well, I figure he'd have to be deaf, blind and stupid to turn down an arrangement like this. John respects you. He knows a good thing when he sees it. You wait and see."

Robert lowered his voice, "I heard the Rose girl wasn't getting along too good. Her mother took her off some place out of town."

"Tyler's all wrapped up in grief over Stephen."

"Damn shame they hadn't married already. She'd of gotten that boy's life insurance."

"I've never known the Roses to hurt for money, Robert. Lawyers and morticians don't usually go hungry. I haven't seen him yet, but I hear Larry's home. Things will be a lot easier for them now."

"Sure will. Lawyers make a sight better money that soldiers."

"I wasn't talking about money, Robert."

"Anybody can use money, Estelle. Hell, we been poor so long you forgot how important money is."

"Oh, I'm sorry, I did forget. Maybe you should remind me. And while you're at it, tell me when we haven't been poor."

Robert groaned quietly. "Don't beat a dead horse, Estelle. We been through that already. Things weren't bad when John lived with us. Not bad at all. And I think once he sees what a help you can be to him, things will pick up again. We may not be on easy street, but there'll be a whole lot less potholes to deal with. I'm sure of it."

Estelle turned on her side and tried to believe it too.

Estelle never expected to like working. It didn't take long though for her to see that it did lend a little spice to her life. She had her hand on the pulse of Bay Harbor. Little went on that she didn't know about. She knew who wrote rubber checks, what kind of nerve medicine the mayor took, and the name of the fat blond who rode to her early job with a married man every morning.

Business was brisk. Johnn needed her. She was convinced of that. He had one girl, Peggy, at the soda fountain, and she wasn't nearly able to wait on customers at the fountain and in other areas of the store at the same time, not with all the new ideas Estelle introduced.

Owens' Drugstore was the first in town to serve banana splits. And the front window had to be filled with timely displays. Estelle had to admit she had a knack for snappy displays. She lined up old windows, complete with curtains, and taped murals behind them as scenes to create the mood of a season. A cardboard cutout of Betty Grable, borrowed from the picture show, stood in front of a display of mouthwash Johnn wanted to move. Who could imagine Betty Grable with bad breath! No, you wouldn't find a stack of blue Kotex boxes decorating the windows of Owens' Drugstore!

People were always complimenting her on some original display, and Estelle found herself spending more time thinking about the displays and goings on at the store than she did on things at home, though there were times when she missed having time to crochet. More and more she began relying on Anna Lee to do the housework and shop for groceries.

Estelle had just finished putting the final touches on a display of cosmetics when, on hands and knees, she backed out of the window. Smoothing her hands over the back of her dress, she held her chin high and walked out the door to view her handiwork.

She ignored her own reflection and looked at the bottles of Evening in Paris cologne that gleamed like jewelry in the morning sun. And the girl's dressing table she'd borrowed from Amy was perfect. The ruffled pink organdy skirt set off the deep blue bottles of cologne she'd arranged there with some Lady Esther face powder, rouge, nail polish, a soft powder puff and pieces of her own dresser set. Amy also let her use a small oriental rug and an antique rocker. Yes, she'd missed her calling all right. Think what she could have done with her talent in Atlanta. Or even Jacksonville! If she was destined to live in a small town, she'd make sure she left her mark on it.

She'd already talked John into selling playing cards and had considerable success with a display of mannequins sitting at a table playing bridge. Actually it was the mannequins she'd borrowed from Stone's dry goods store that were the success.

People in Bay Harbor had never seen mannequins used to advertise anything but clothes, and here were four ladies playing a leisurely hand of bridge. Estelle tried to give them characteristics of local people. She mixed things up, of course, not wanting to be too obvious, but people noticed. One wore a saucy hat but no shoes. Another had a cigarette holder wedged between her fingers. A male mannequin looked over the shoulder of another. Things like that. And all the women began trying to guess who the people were, and they brought their husbands to get their opinions as well.

People lingered before that display more than any other, enough that they drew the attention of the Baptist minister. When he denounced the sin of card playing and called upon his congregation to boycott both the dry goods store and drugstore in protest, Mr. Stone sent a clerk to retrieve the mannequins. He claimed he needed them for a special display, but Estelle knew different. It was a real shame. The bridge partner she'd referred to privately as Mrs. Stone was the most fetching of all.

Lost in thought, Estelle stood before the window longer than usual. She realized she'd quit looking at the display and was preening a bit, concentrating on her red dress with chevron stripes, and her newly permed hair. Embarrassed, she turned around to see if anyone was watching. It didn't appear she'd been noticed so she fluffed her hair and turned back to the window. She put her hand over her mouth to stifle a scream. There in the window, in her own display, Hilton Fields grinned at her from the antique rocker.

Hilton gripped the arms of the rocker and started to get up when Estelle lifted her right hand, palm out, signaling him to stop. She liked a surprise as much as the next person so she raised her forefinger and mouthed, "Wait."

She ran across the street and cut between the Piggly Wiggly and Daniel's Furniture Store to the next block. She knew her chances of catching Robert at the station were slim, but she wanted to try. She slowed down to ease her racing heart when she saw his car parked in front. *Metal outhouse,* she thought, as she stepped through the door. Robert was standing, talking to the Chief of Police. The chief was sitting in a straight chair tilted backward on two legs against the wall. He was a big man, and Estelle laughed. "You put a lot of faith in the chair, Buster."

He nodded, taking a toothpick from his mouth. "And to what do we owe the pleasure of your company, Estelle?"

A sheen of moisture on his ruddy, wide-pored face made her slightly nauseous but she smiled and said, "I need Robert to come with me for a few minutes, Buster."

Robert hitched up his pants. "Estelle, you know I cain't just leave work. If you've got business, tell me. Somebody rob the drugstore?"

"Nobody robbed anything that I know of, but there'll be a murder if you don't come with me now!"

Buster laughed and let his chair drop forward. His cheeks puffed out, and he hit his chest with his fist. "Damn them sausages they serve at the boarding house." He reached over and took a box of Arm and Hammer baking soda from the desk drawer. Half a glass of water sat on the desk, and with a practiced move, he held the box over the glass and tapped it with his forefinger. "Better get out of here, Robert. I'm in no shape for a murder right now." He stirred the water with his finger.

Robert adjusted his felt hat, pulling the brim forward, and walked out the door ahead of Estelle.

"Wait, Robert, so I can walk with you." Estelle stepped on the cement block that served as a step and rushed after him.

"Just stay back, Estelle. This way it looks like official business and not a walk in the park."

Estelle wasn't happy about it, but she kept her distance. Robert looked back over his shoulder. "What's this all about?"

"I want you to see my new display."

Robert stopped so suddenly she almost ran into him. "I cain't believe what you just said. Sweet Jesus! You take me off the job to see a window display!"

"You weren't working and you know it. You can give me five minutes of your time when I spend hours every day working to put food on the table."

Robert's face went white with rage, and Estelle knew she'd gone too far.

"I put food on the table, Estelle. You help out. I still wear the pants in this family. Hell fire! I just cain't believe you called me out here to see a window display. It better be damn good."

"Oh, it is, Robert. It is."

As they approached the drugstore, they could see a group of people gathered in front of the window, and Estelle smiled. She heard somebody call, "Here comes the sheriff."

Robert looked at the people who started to disperse as he came closer. He didn't turn toward the window until the last minute. His body grew still, ramrod straight. Hilton sat in the rocker reading *Life* magazine, a pipe in the corner of his mouth.

When Hilton saw Robert he stood up, and the magazine fell to the floor. He smiled and held up two fingers in a V. In turn, Robert saluted, his eyes bright with unshed tears. He still hadn't moved when Hilton jumped down from the window and came outside where Robert waited, his body rigid with repressed emotion. They stood a few feet apart, just staring at each other for a moment before Hilton grabbed Robert in a bear hug.

Estelle and her window display were totally ignored. She hadn't expected Robert to notice. But she did think Hilton would say something.

Estelle felt a pang of jealously and the heat of anger over this tender reunion. She knew Hilton and Robert had been thick as thieves at one time. They shared a whole history that didn't include her.

How could I have been so stupid as to arrange a meeting of old friends like this, playing right into Hilton's hands. I'm nothing but a pawn, and now I damn well better figure a way to get Hilton to leave town at the earliest possible moment. Bay Harbor doesn't need the likes of Hilton Fields. He never could keep his pants zipped.

CHAPTER
Seven

April 1946

Seven months without war ushered a welcome April into Bay Harbor with the promise of new growth, peace, and hope for the future. The palm trees were green with renewal, geraniums and roses were blooming, the air clean and fresh.

Her bedroom windows opened wide to the breeze, Emily Richards leaned down to look at her reflection in the old three-piece mirror on her dressing table. She tucked a strand of silver hair into her bun and thought the mirror shifted. She caught the side of the table and steadied herself. She hated these pesky dizzy spells and tried to remember if she'd asked Annie to prepare lunch. Straightening, she approached the stairs with careful steps. Perhaps it was time to have her bedroom moved to the first floor.

The dining table was polished and set with woven placemats and Havilland china. She heard Annie in the kitchen preparing lunch. She straightened one of the linen napkins and turned to see Hilton coming downstairs.

"I'm having lunch with Robert."

"But, Hilton," she began and gestured toward the two place settings.

"Mother, I told you it wasn't necessary to prepare meals for me."

"I know but . . ." she turned to walk away.

"I'm sorry." He kissed her cheek and whispered, "Have you forgotten I'm not good at conversation, even for lunch?" He looked at the table. "No point in going to all this trouble."

"No trouble, dear. I'm sure Annie won't mind." Her tone implied it mattered to her, but she straightened her shoulders and walked to the kitchen. *Let him take offense. He always did.*

Hilton hesitated at the front door, tempted to say something more, but he didn't want to betray his anger. They were always at sixes and sevens. He'd returned from the war to find her widowed once more. She told him she hadn't wanted to burden him with that bit of information while he was overseas. Didn't she realize she made him feel more like a stranger than ever? He'd never wanted to live in the same town with her, but hoped now that she was older, they could work things out.

Hilton hadn't told Robert they were having lunch and was rushing to catch him in time or he would have stopped at the Baptist Church and bought something from their bake sale. As it was, he pulled in at the police station just as Robert was walking to his car.

"Hey, you got plans for dinner?" Hilton knew the noon meal would be dinner for Robert.

"Since Estelle started work, it's catch as catch can, son."

"Let's go to the oyster bar then." He'd hardly finished speaking when Robert was in the car beside him.

"If I didn't know better, I'd think you liked oysters." Robert smiled and put his hat on the seat between them.

"How come you're eating out?"

"I've decided to take life easy, enjoy myself. Seems like I've been buying property and moving my investments around most of my life. All I've done is make money. Now I want to spend some of it."

"I hope that means you're paying."

Hilton laughed. "Thank God you never change. Remember when we were kids how you always daydreamed about inheriting money from your grandmother?"

"I remember. And when she died everything she had went to Johnn, and that was precious little, believe me."

"Except for the war, I feel like I haven't done a thing with my life but try to make money."

"You got a head for it. You bought stocks and property on the cheap, stuff that seemed like it weren't worth nothing, and their value always multiplied. Everything you touched turned to gold."

Hilton laughed. "You were the one always wanting money. Lord knows but we were poor, especially after Daddy died. I've often wondered if it was your craving for wealth, you always hoping to inherit something that fueled my drive to be rich."

"Damn shame it didn't fuel mine. I'm still waiting for my ship to come in."

"Keep your eyes peeled. It might be in the harbor."

Robert snorted. "I'd need glasses to see that far away."

They pulled up to the oyster bar and when Robert started to open the door, Hilton put his hand on his arm to stop him. "I've decided to make Bay Harbor my home. I'm going to settle down here."

"Well, god damn." Robert stared at Hilton openmouthed and blinked hard. "The women in Bay Harbor better watch out."

Hilton laughed. "I can hear your stomach growling. Let's put away some oysters."

Hilton watched Robert eat, hardly able to contain his euphoria, stopping short of telling Robert he wanted to embrace the whole town and everybody in it. For him Bay Harbor was a song, a place, a dream. This was his new beginning, a place where he could be a different person, maybe even a better man.

When they left the oyster bar, Hilton pulled Robert to the side and they walked along the Bay. "Look out there, Robert. You see anything?"

"The sun shining on the water."

"Well, look again. I think your ship's coming in."

"Not likely, son. Estelle's working and bills are still piling up."

Hilton picked up an oyster shell and threw it into the Bay. "How'd you like to work for your best friend?"

"Huh?"

"You heard me. I need somebody to go on the road for me, keep an eye on my properties, make my payroll."

"Aw, Hil, I'd love to, but you know I got a family."

"You'd be home every weekend. If there's a problem, Estelle can call on me any hour of the day or night. And, Robert, I'll make it more than worth your while. I'll pay you more than you're making now and in ten years, if times are good, fifteen if the economy slows, I'll deed over some shares of stock and two hundred acres of prime land, one of my farms and some rich pine forests."

"Hil," Robert's voice choked. "Hil," he started again, "I don't know how many surprises I can take in one day. It was enough jes to know you planned to settle down here, but now you've gone and offered to make me a man of means." Robert shook his head and walked down the shore, away from Hilton.

To be the big man. No waiting in line for a check but handing out checks, sitting behind a desk for Christ sake. He stared at the reflection of the sun rippling on the Bay and blinked back tears. He didn't see a ship, he saw a memory. Flames licking up over a campfire.

Robert squinted, seeing the boy Hilton leaning forward toward fire, intent on something Robert was saying. Hilton had never liked to hunt, had never fired a gun in his life until he was drafted, but when he was young Robert knew Hilton went hunting with him just to keep him company, just so they could be together around the campfire, something his own twin brother wouldn't do for him. Earl never enjoyed hunting the way Robert did, was never quite comfortable around guns, and was more than happy to have Hilton take his place.

In the dark, in the privacy of the woods, Hilton confided his worst fears. He suffered being a disappointment to his mother, but most of his fears concerned women. He was little more than a boy when they began noticing him in ways that made him uneasy.

"Nothing to be uneasy about Hil," Robert told him. "Jes enjoy it. Let them put a crown on your head if they want to." If it'd been anybody but Hilton, Robert would have been jealous. After all, he was somewhat of a looker himself. As it was, the two of them sat around the fire, Hilton telling Robert the things women did. Later Robert would find some pretext to go calling. "You find the ripe berries, Hil, and I'll do the picking."

He had to admit Hilton found them in some pretty unlikely places. Once Hilton's mother sent him to McCormick's Grocery to pay her bill when she was sick with the flu. There was a sign on the door saying the store was closed for the day so Hilton walked around to the back of the building where the McCormicks lived. His mother had always told him a schoolteacher could never afford to be behind in her bills so he figured he'd better pay her bill no matter what.

Mrs. McCormick came to the door and said her husband was sick with the same flu that had Hilton's mother in bed.

"I'd never paid her no mind before, Robert, 'cept to feel sorry for her being married to a blind man. She was just an older woman, same as Mother. But that morning I paid attention.

"She was in her bathrobe, a shaggy old blue chenille that wasn't closed in front. For an older woman she looked good."

"Is that right?" Robert picked up a stick and jabbed the fire.

"Yeah, real good. She stood in front of me for a long time. What else could I do but look? I couldn't talk cause my mouth was too dry. Her brassiere and panties was some pink silky material. She was breathing hard and everythin' she had on was a moving up and down. Felt like I'd been there an hour before Mr. McCormick began hollering for her. I held the money out, and she put her palm under mine, like this." Hilton grabbed Robert's hand. "And then ever so slowly," he raked his palm over Robert's, "she slid the money off my hand."

"Her hands were cool and soft, and I think Mr. McCormick's a lucky man even if he is blind."

Things like that were always happening to Hilton. Women like to touch him, to have him look at them. Something as simple as a paper route became torturous.

Going to collect he'd find them in filmy negligees and little else. "One day, Robert, a woman come to the door in shorts, then seemed to think better of herself, and right there in front of me she buttoned a wrap skirt over her bare legs, smiling all the time."

"So? I've seen lots of women in shorts, Hil."

"Yeah, Robert, but she didn't have nothing on up top. Nothing. I never saw anything so beautiful. I was hurtin', really I was, and then she leaned forward to hand me the money." Hilton paused and drew a deep breath. "I didn't move and neither did her . . . you know. They might have been painted on her body. I almost touched her. Next time I might." Terrified for his future, Hilton quit his paper route.

Robert hadn't wanted him to quit, loved hearing these stories, but he didn't pressure him one way or the other. There were plenty of other avenues to women but only one Hilton.

"You see that ship yet, partner?"

Robert jumped. "What? Oh, the ship." He took out a can of Prince Albert and tapped some tobacco onto a cigarette paper. "I was lost in thought, Hil, thinking about when we was kids. You know, son, I think I do see it. It's a pretty damn big boat too. Course, I got to see if I can get Estelle to come on board."

"Take your time. Don't want you to jump into anythin' you're not sure about."

"I'm sure. It's just convincing Estelle. She's jealous of the times we had when we was young, of our friendship now that you're here."

"Robert, you sorry knocker, what good's a friendship that can't strike a spark of envy in a jealous wife? We've got more than friendship. We've got a bond. Just impress on her what this'll mean in the long run. She may be full of vinegar, but she's not dumb."

"That's what I'm countin' on, Hil. That's what I'm countin' on."

When they arrived back at the police station, Hilton reached for his billfold and counted out a fifty and five twenty dollar bills.

"Is this a bribe?"

Hilton laughed. "No, I want you to go over to the Baptist church and buy something fancy for Estelle to have for dessert tonight."

"I don't think they got anything that fancy, Hil."

"No. But they need the money. They want to repave their parking lot, and that's one hell of a lot of cake and cookies. Just don't tell them where this came from."

"What if they think it's from me?"

Hilton laughed again. "I doubt they'll think that, you old sinner. Hell, you couldn't find your way up the church steps if you tried."

"Not with all them hypocrites."

"Like I said, they won't think it's from you."

By one-thirty Hilton was back at his mother's, starving. He'd gone to the oyster bar for Robert.

He stood on the front steps gazing out toward the Bay. He was restless with an uncomfortable, unfamiliar nervousness in his gut that had nothing to do with hunger.

His mother called from the balcony. "Are you going or coming, Hilton?" He flushed with anger. *Hold on. Don't let her spoil your dream.*

"Both, Mother. Just thought I'd take a walk out on the pier. The Bay looks calm as glass, and it's such a warm day."

"I wish I felt up to coming with you."

With a pang of guilt Hilton realized he was glad she wasn't up to it. "Yes, Mother, I wish you did too. You know, I think I'll pack a lunch and eat out there."

"But I thought you had lunch with Robert."

His jaw stiffened. *Why does she always make me feel like a naughty child?* "It was more Robert having lunch. We went to an oyster bar, and I still have a hard time getting raw oysters down. It'll be relaxing to eat on the pier."

"You'll find cold cuts for sandwiches in the refrigerator and some fresh tomatoes on the counter. There's a gracious plenty of cold drinks too. I can't get used to such luxuries now that the war's over, and I end up buying too much of everything. I guess I'll get used to it eventually." She looked down, but Hilton had already gone back inside the house. She sank to a chair and rested her elbows on the gracefully curved railing of the balcony.

When Hilton came outside again her eyes followed his departing figure. Tears blurred her vision, and she didn't see he'd stopped in the middle of the walk. At first he just stood there and then turned and looked up to where she was sitting.

He held up a sack and a bottle of Coca Cola. "I helped myself to some cold chicken. Hope you didn't have plans for it."

"No, no plans, dear. Hilton?"

"Ma'am?"

"It's wonderful to have you here. You don't know how I've lived for this day."

"I've lived for it too."

"Be careful. The pier isn't what it was before the war. The wood's rotting and boards are missing."

His face hardened. *All these years, and she still played the cautious schoolteacher.* "Mother, I came through a war. I believe I can . . ."

She interrupted him. "Yes, dear, but you always hear of people living through terrible times and then being killed in some little freak accident. I just wanted you to be aware. You aren't from around here, you know."

"I was lots of places during the war that I wasn't from, places a lot more dangerous than a rotting pier." Seeing how thin and faded she looked, he was instantly ashamed. "I'm sorry. I appreciate your concern. I'll be off before this drink gets hot." Under his breath, he muttered, "Miss Emmie," the pet name her students had given her.

By the time he reached the pier Hilton knew he had to hurry things up and get out of his mother's house. He hoped Robert wouldn't waste any time making his appeal to Estelle.

He looked down. His mother was right. The pier certainly was in bad shape. In places as many as three planks were missing, and he had to jump from board to board. The side rails were gone entirely. The covered portion at the end of the walkway seemed to be in somewhat better condition. Hilton had thought it was deserted but then saw a girl with her back to him, legs dangling over the edge of the platform. She'd tilted her head backward, and lifted her face to the sun. Hilton didn't say anything, just eased himself to a bench and took a long swig of coke.

With hands behind her, palms flat on the platform, she offered her jutting breasts to the sun as well. She wore a thin blouse, but Hilton got a pretty good idea of what she looked like without it.

He forgot all about the glassy surface of the Bay. Every now and then the wind lifted her blouse and he could see a flash of golden skin. He envisioned it lifting the blouse to reveal her breasts as well, imagining the familiar feel of her nipple on his lips.

And then the sweating bottle slipped from his unsteady hand and fell to the floor with a loud thud. "Shit!"

The girl jumped and fell forward. Afraid she'd fall into the water, Hilton rushed over and grabbed her arm.

She was totally flustered and maybe a little afraid. He saw she had undone several buttons of her blouse, and his eyes lingered there. He let go of her arm and she scooted backward onto the pier, holding her skirt down in the breeze off the water.

"I'm sorry. Didn't mean to frighten you. You were so relaxed, half asleep, I didn't want to disturb you, and then the fool drink slipped out of my hand."

She closed her slanting green eyes and smiled so that he didn't feel so bad about scaring her. Gene Tierney, that's who she looked like. A naughty Gene Tierney.

"I'm Hilton Fields. My mother, Emily Richards, lives across the street." He pointed to the two story house with white columns and pink tile roof.

"I'm Tyler. Tyler Rose."

"To show you I really am sorry, come over here and share my picnic with me. Will you do that? I raided Mother's refrigerator so there's more than enough for the two of us."

"Thank you. I'd like that."

She picked up her shoes and followed him across the warm boards to the bench on the far side of the platform. There was a slight bead of perspiration on her upper lip Hilton would like to have taken credit for, but she had been sunbathing after all.

He held the open bag out to her, and she took a leg. "First real warm day we've had in awhile, isn't it?"

She smiled and nodded but made no attempt to do a thing about her blouse. He'd learned a lot about women when he was a paperboy. Had she forgotten or was she inviting him to look?

"So you're a Rose. Your folks own the funeral home?"

"I'm so sick of everything coming back to the funeral home! It's like a cross I carry on my back!"

Hilton whistled. "I didn't mean to step on anybody's toes."

"I'm sorry. It's just a sore spot with me. My Uncle Foster runs the funeral home. Daddy . . . my dad is a lawyer. Or he was before the war. He isn't the same since he got home."

"Not many of us are."

"But he wants to work with my uncle now, doing personality sketches for tombstones." Her golden skin burned copper, and she tossed her hair back away from her face. "If I smoked I'd want a cigarette right now. Sorry, I don't mean to air the family linen. It's just that my mother is very upset about this, but it seems all he can do right now. It's a ghoulish business if you ask me. But nobody asks."

"Well, it's a far cry from being a lawyer. I can sympathize with your mother. I was in the Pacific. The war did strange things to people."

"Did it do strange things to you?"

"Yes, I'd have to say it did, to all of us. After all, just about every misfit who could manage to walk and talk and focus his eyes was in the war."

"Did that include you?" Her voice was soft but deep.

"No. I'm very coordinated," Hilton responded as he leaned forward and began buttoning her blouse. She flinched and uttered a small, "Oh!" but didn't pull back or say anything.

Tyler never took her eyes off his hands, nor did she say anything about their slight tremor. "My fiancé never took such liberties, Mr. Fields."

"I find that hard to believe, not with someone as beautiful as you."

She narrowed her eyes and looked at him for a long minute. "I don't know if I should thank you or slap you."

"It's your call, lady. Just trying to be helpful." He raised his eyebrows and gave her a wicked smile.

"I'll take you at your word then. Thank you, Mr. Fields."

"The pleasure was all mine, Miss Rose."

Her gaze met his and held a moment. Then Tyler stood, making fists to keep her hands from shaking. "I really should be going. Nice meeting you."

"Again, the pleasure was all mine."

"Well, goodbye now." She started away and stopped. She kept her back to him. "I didn't remember that my blouse was unbuttoned. I'm not forward."

"That's too bad. I was about to invite you to a movie."

Tyler didn't move, but when he said nothing more, she walked away, stepping over gaping holes in the uncovered walkway.

Hilton laughed to himself. *Well, it's started. Engaged or not, she's definitely interested.*

CHAPTER
Eight

Tyler didn't know how much longer she could stand hearing her parents argue. It was the same thing every night when she went to bed and every morning when she woke up.

"Larry, you've set all the tongues to wagging. What do you suppose people think? All these years you've been their lawyer, and they're beholden to you for going off to war. But the war's over, Larry. It's over."

"Can't you understand it'll never be over for me, Beatrice?"

"Well, it's still over, and you're home. Home, Larry, and you haven't darkened the door of your office."

"Beatrice, I have an office at the funeral home. I have files. I'm not practicing law, but I am working. If you don't believe me, come over some day and see for yourself. You must be the only person in town who's unhappy with my mission in life."

"Your mission, Larry? You call that a mission?"

"Yes, I do. If I can put a picture on a tombstone that captures the essence of someone's time on this earth, I call that a mission."

Beatrice slapped her pillow against the headboard and sat up in bed. "I'll never go over there, and you will never make me believe God wants you to give up a good education to play around with tombstones."

Tyler buried her head under a pillow. How could she think about the man she'd met on the pier with them shouting at each other? With her face covered she felt along her nightstand with her right hand. She found the frame holding Stephen's picture and turned it face down.

She liked to relive every minute she'd been on the pier with Hilton, most of all when he buttoned her blouse. Her body's reaction to that simple gesture taught her something about herself she hadn't known before. She enjoyed having a man touch her in a sensuous way. Even a stranger.

The next morning Tyler waited until Larry left the house before she got up. She took a bubble bath, wrapped her hair in a towel, and stood in front of her closet for a long time. She discarded several outfits before selecting a white rayon blouse with long fitted sleeves and a wide belted aqua skirt with un-pressed pleats. She liked the new draped look even if it was a bit dressy for a trip to the furniture store. What did she care. She was dressing for Hilton, knew that for the rest of her life she'd dress the way she'd want to look for him.

Beatrice had become more and more reluctant to leave the house so it fell to Tyler to buy a new lamp for the living room. Her dad had fallen asleep on the couch one night and broke a table lamp when he flailed about in one of his nightmares.

"You're mighty dressed up today," Beatrice commented, as she counted out money for a lamp. "But I'm glad. You look nice. Cheerful."

Tyler noticed that her mother's eyes were red from crying, but she didn't know what she could say to make things better. It had all been said a hundred times. She brushed her mother's cheek with a kiss and left.

She forced herself to walk to the funeral home and out back to her dad's office. They hadn't been as close since he returned from the war, and she missed that. She found him going through a file, and papers were spread over his desk. He looked up when she came in and for a moment he appeared stunned, as though he didn't recognize her.

"Daddy?"

"Oh, Tyler! You don't usually come over here. I didn't expect you. You look nice, very nice."

"Thanks." She smiled and tired to keep her voice light, social. "Just thought I'd see how you're doing. You work every Saturday?"

"For now anyway. I'm fine, darling. Believe it or not, I'm very busy. I hadn't anticipated so much interest in tombstone renderings, not this soon anyway. Word got around a lot quicker than I expected."

"It's more than that. You talk to people, take an interest in their lives. And you listen. You always did. It's not often people get that kind of attention."

"I guess not. I've learned one thing. Even in death men and women want different things. The men are all worried that I might put something on a tombstone that doesn't capture their true essence. They tell me who they really are. The women who come to the office aren't so interested in how they'll be remembered as the possibilities of creating a new vision while there's still time, and they expect me to help them figure out what they should be doing with their lives."

"I guess that's what I'm trying to do, create a new vision for my life."

"Oh, darling." Larry got up and wrapped her in his arms. "I'm so sorry. You know I'd take your pain if I could."

"I know, but losing Stephen is something I have to live with. Nobody can do it for me."

"That's true, but it's a tough way to grow up."

Tyler looked at him. One eye drooped a little, but they were still bright blue, his blond hair was thick and his arms muscular. Despite all he'd been through he was a handsome man. He and her mother seemed such an unlikely couple, more so now than ever.

"And, Tyler, I'm sorry about all this." He extended his right arm toward the pictures pinned to the wall, the sketch pads on his desk, broken pieces of charcoal and colored pencils. "I just have to be here."

"I know you do. With time it'll work out. It has to."

"Thanks, honey. And thanks for coming by."

Tyler was just walking out the door when he called to her. "You know, your friend Anna Lee takes more interest in my work than anyone else."

"Anna Lee?"

"Yeah. Seldom a day she isn't over here. I asked her if she wanted to be a mortician, and she said no, she'd like to do what I'm doing."

"She's never mentioned it to me, but I know she and T. J. are friends."

"That explains it then. She's probably trying to get one up on T. J."

Tyler laughed. "That would take some doing. See you tonight, Daddy."

Tyler was testing the texture of a lampshade between her thumb and forefinger when she looked out the window and saw Hilton standing beneath the awning in front of the post office. Judging from the pleased look on his face, he might've been the happiest man alive. He wore brown slacks and one finger held a tan jacket behind his right shoulder, the other hand in his pocket. He was looking up at the deep blue sky, smiling.

She had to go to him. Powerless not to. Tyler forgot her purse beside the lamp and walked out the door without a word to anyone. She was sure she hadn't drawn a breath but walked straight to Hilton, angling right at the last minute to pass him and walk into the post office. No one had ever affected her in just that way, and he didn't appear to have even noticed her. He continued looking skyward.

She stood in the middle of the post office lobby for a moment and then seemed to come out of a trance. Several people looked at her indulgently, the way they had since Stephen . . . *Oh, poor Stephen.* She turned back toward the door and saw Anna Lee stop and speak to Hilton before he walked away.

Anna Lee came inside saying, "Seven to the right twice, twenty to the left twice, and . . ."

Tyler looked puzzled. "What are you doing?"

"It's the combination to our mailbox. I like saying it."

"You're weird, you know that?" Her voice was harsh and unfriendly as she stared at her, ignoring the tears Anna Lee tried to blink back.

"I guess so, but Lola says I have to start acting more grownup because I'll be thirteen soon."

"The lighthouse keeper's daughter said that?"

"Lola wants me to improve myself."

"Is she some kind of authority?"

"Oh, yes. She knows everything about manners."

"Does she know who you were talking to outside?"

"Uh huh."

"How do you know him?"

"Cause he's Daddy's best friend in all the world. They grew up together in Tallahassee."

Tyler could hardly contain her excitement. "Maybe we can be best friends too, Anna Lee."

"You said I was weird."

"Well if I did, on you it's becoming."

"You're just saying that."

"I'd never do that to my best friend. Come on, help me pick out a lamp. We have lots to talk about."

Anna Lee felt a swelling pride in her chest, forgetting that only yesterday Tyler had called her weird. The shoe was on the other foot now. It wasn't just Tyler and Lola being important to her. She'd become special to them.

Lola insisted she wanted Anna Lee to practice making introductions and had asked that she introduce her to Hilton one day when they saw him in the drugstore. Anna Lee knew that for once Lola wasn't thinking about manners at all. And now Tyler was showing an interest in Hilton too. At last she had something these girls wanted.

Mrs. Edwards had driven up to the house earlier that morning, and Lola came in and said she had some clothes she'd outgrown. Maybe Anna Lee would like to come by the lighthouse and see if anything fit her.

Anna Lee had planned to spend some time with T. J. but couldn't turn down an offer like that. She didn't care if anyone recognized them as hand-me-downs. Lola's clothes were all store bought.

She went by the drugstore to let her mother know she was on the way to the lighthouse. "Anna Lee, I'd just had an idea for a new window display and now you made me forget."

"Lola says she has some clothes that might fit me."

At that Estelle broke into a smile. "Isn't that nice of her to think of you? I surely don't have time to do much sewing any more. Don't worry if they're too big. You'll grow into them."

"Yes ma'am."

When she got to the lighthouse Lola offered her a pink sweater with matching cardigan, a silvery blue raincoat with a hood, and a red and gray plaid skirt. The raincoat was much too long, but Lola assured her that Estelle could take it up easy enough. Anna Lee folded the skirt and sweater without trying them on.

"I'll grow into them," she muttered. She wouldn't give the sweater set up for the world. If only it came with Lola's bust built in.

Lola's eyes sparkled. "Come in the kitchen. Mother just made a pitcher of tea, and look at the bowl of apples Dad brought back from Charleston. Aren't they pretty? They're made of wax so don't go trying to eat one.

Anna Lee nodded. "I like the way you call her mother. I've noticed that only rich girls have mothers. The rest of us have mamas."

Lola laughed. "We aren't rich."

"You act rich."

"Well then you can act rich too."

"I doubt it. I don't look rich."

"We'll work on it. You have to learn to be more ladylike."

She set a glass of iced tea in front of Anna Lee. "Are you singing at the table!"

"Just humming *Don't Sit Under the Apple Tree*."

"Well, it's all the same. Well brought up young ladies don't sing or hum at the table."

"That bowl of apples made me think of it."

"Are you sure you're going to be thirteen? That's a romantic song. Food shouldn't remind you of romance. What does Night and Day make you think of?"

"Night and Day?"

"You know, 'Night and day you are the one . . .'" she sang, still standing, Anna Lee noted, not sitting at the table.

Anna Lee tried her best to think of something romantic.

"Well?"

"Hilton. It makes me think of Hilton," she lied. She almost said bedtime.

Lola broke into a big smile, and Anna Lee knew she had the right answer. "Very good, Anna Lee. I wouldn't at all mind thinking of him night and day."

Her mother spoke up from the next room, her voice cold. "You better watch who you think about, Miss Priss. How do you know Mr. Fields?"

"Anna Lee introduced us. He's always so friendly."

"I bet he is. He's old enough to be your father."

"Uh uh. He smiled at me the other day, and I nearly fainted. And how do you know him anyway?"

Virginia came into the room and Anna Lee noticed a flush of pink splotches creeping up her neck.

"I don't live in a cave, you know. I saw him in the drugstore getting medicine for Mrs. Richards."

"He looks young to me. How old is he, Anna Lee?"

"I don't know. Mama says he won't tell anybody. I know he isn't as old at Daddy even if they are best friends, but that's all I know."

Lola whispered. "Can you imagine having a date with him?"

Anna Lee shook her head. Hilton was a family friend, not somebody she'd ever think about dating. "What would you talk to him about?"

"The war, I guess. And I could ask about his mother. I've been reading Emily Post so I know all about etiquette. I'd like him to take me to a fancy restaurant where everyone would see us."

"You'd have to go to the boarding house or to Frenchie's for a hamburger. There aren't any fancy restaurants in Bay Harbor."

Lola threw her head back and looked at Anna Lee critically. "No," she drawled, exhaling the word like smoke from a long cigarette, "but don't you think it would be nice to be prepared when you encounter these situations? Do you never expect to leave this town? And don't forget that there are some nice homes in Bay Harbor, places where elegant meals are served."

Anna Lee knew she was thinking of Hilton's mother. Who could imagine Mrs. Richards eating in the kitchen? One could very well see her, though, sitting at one end of a long, polished dining room table, Hilton at the other.

Lola got up and dumped some chicken broth into a pan to warm. "Now just imagine, Anna Lee, that you were invited to dinner at a really elegant home. Would you know which fork to use?" Without waiting for an answer, she said, "I would." She tapped her temple with a forefinger. "Emily Post. The only thing that worries me is olives."

"Olives?"

"Yes. What in the world would you do with an olive pit? You couldn't just spit it on your plate."

"Why not?"

"Anna Lee, you are hopeless. Think how it would look. And if you spit it in your spoon, that would just draw attention to the awful, gnawed thing. Just imagine everyone staring at you as you lowered your spoon from your mouth to your plate."

Anna Lee brightened. "Why couldn't you just spit it in your napkin?"

Lola looked at her with disgust. "Anne Lee, in really nice places, they don't use paper napkins. How would it look to pick up a linen napkin and find an olive pit in it? It'd be like finding a hair ball. It might even roll to the floor and you'd have to pick it up."

"If they're that fine, they'd have a maid to do it. What would a maid care?"

"It's what you'd imply by doing something like that. No, I think it'd be best to discretely spit the pit into your hand and place it on your plate when no one is looking."

"Well, I sure won't eat olives." Anna Lee made a face. "You could sit there holding an olive pit for hours."

"I will. I'll eat olives and anything else they serve. And when I get married, I'll always have finger bowls on the table."

"You'll have to wash a lot of dishes then."

"Maybe I'll just have a maid, you know." Lola placed two soup bowls on the table and filled them with broth. "Now we'll practice eating soup properly."

"But we've done that before."

"I want to see if you can do it this time without slurping. And don't make waves in the soup bowl either."

They slid their spoons through bowls of broth, a forward movement and then sipped quietly from the side of the spoon. Anna Lee knew she'd never enjoy a bowl of soup again. She wasn't even sure she wanted to be a lady any more.

The minute Virginia came back into the room she jumped up and poured her remaining broth down the sink.

"Did Lola tell you we're going to have a big party for her sixteenth birthday?"

"Is that what we're practicing for?"

"I don't think so, darling." Virginia squeezed Anna Lee's shoulder.

Lola lifted her long auburn hair with the back of her hand as though to cool her neck. "Mother and I have been planning it for weeks. It's going to be a dance."

"I don't know how to dance."

"I can't invite you anyway. You're too young."

"Maybe she could help me serve," Virginia offered.

"Mother!" Lola sounded exasperated but then her face brightened. "It'll be in the evening, Anna Lee. Maybe you could ask Hilton to give you a ride here. I have a beautiful new dress."

"Mr. Fields to you, Lola."

Anna Lee hesitated. "I don't know. Are you having soup and olives?"

"Oh, stop it," Lola chided. "We're having lime punch, petit fours, mixed nuts, ginger ale, and potato chips."

"You aren't going to have a cake?"

Lola closed her eyes in exasperation. "That's what petit fours are, Anna Lee. Little cakes."

"Which fork do you eat them with?"

"Petit fours are eaten with your fingers."

"Could you fit a whole one in your mouth?"

"I've never tried and you better not either. Not at my party!"

"Then it's settled." Virginia smiled. "You can help me serve, baby."

CHAPTER
Nine

Friday Night – May 1946

Larry lay flat on his back in the darkness, wondering if he'd ever have a peaceful night's sleep again. Each night, as soon as the lights were out Beatrice started complaining.

He sighed. "I'm sorry, Bea. I know this isn't what you bargained for, but I can't help it. If you want me to leave, I will."

"Leave? Where would you go?"

"I could fix a place at Foster's. He wouldn't mind."

"I don't want you to leave, Larry. I just want our old life back."

"I wish I could give it to you, Bea. I really do. Just the way you want it, but I can't. Not now. Maybe never."

"Never?" He heard the catch in her voice and wondered if she was going to start crying again. He wished he could take her in his arms and comfort her, but he couldn't. It was easier to chisel pictures on tombstones than it was to love Bea.

How had they come to this? Would he still feel the same if he hadn't met Heather? At one time he'd felt protective toward Bea, had wanted to comfort her. It seemed now that was all there'd ever been. Just a need to protect her.

Foster hadn't wanted him to marry Bea in the first place. Begged him not to. Too late Larry realized he should have listened, but he had grown accustomed to distancing himself from his younger brother.

Foster had been their father's favorite. He was tall, broad shouldered, perpetually happy, eager to follow in his father's footsteps and become an undertaker.

The first-born son, Larry was Lawrence, Jr., but it felt like a putdown. He was junior to everything, especially Foster. Foster wearing a football sweater, Foster sitting on the front steps strumming a ukulele, girls at his feet, guy friends eager for his approval. Everybody wanted to be Foster's friend, everybody but Larry.

Foster was right though. Larry hadn't really known Bea that well. She was older, ran with a different crowd, and later he was away at college.

Foster had always dated more, and Larry knew that where women were concerned, Foster tried to look out for him.

Home from school one Christmas, Foster urged him to leave his books and come to a party. Larry hadn't wanted to go, but Foster insisted. And Beatrice was there. Loud and brash. That was Bea. Larry thought she was interesting and later would counter Foster's arguments with, "She made a 'Bea' line for me. How could I resist?"

They argued about it incessantly. "You don't have enough experience, Larry. You should date lots of girls. Believe me, there are plenty of 'em out there who'd suit you better than Beatrice Stevens. She's older than you, for God's sake . . . And louder and . . ."

"Not all that much. She's old enough to make a good wife. To be ready to settle down. And, Foster, she hangs onto every word I say. She's interested in me."

"She's grateful."

"What?"

"Grateful. The ugly ones always are."

"She's not ugly."

"If you don't think so then this must be true love."

"Don't be unkind. Her parents being killed in that wreck. She's all alone in the world."

"Yeah, and why's that? Cause her old man had a drinking problem, that's why. Do you want a wife who's an alcoholic? Do you want ugly children?"

Well, Foster hadn't been completely right. Beatrice never touched a drop of liquor, and Tyler was anything but ugly. But deep in his heart, Larry knew there'd been a lot of truth in what Foster had been trying to tell him.

He hadn't had enough experience, was ripe for the picking. He'd wanted to take care of Bea. Too late he realized she hadn't needed taking care of. After they were married, it became more and more evident that what Bea wanted was the legitimacy of being a lawyer's wife rather than the daughter of the town drunk. Under the guise of helping Larry get established professionally, it became very important to Bea that they be seen with the right people, have invitations to the popular parties.

Maybe he was being unfair. He forced himself to reach over and take her hand. They didn't speak. After awhile she pulled her hand away and turned away from him, lay on her side, facing the wall.

"You haven't touched me once since you've been home. I haven't asked you to tell me, but sometimes it makes me wonder . . ."

"I'm sorry. It isn't you. It's . . ."

She sighed. "I know. It's the war. Are you going to go on blaming the war forever?"

"I don't know. You weren't there. You can't imagine what it was like, the things I'll never forget. Things I bring to bed with me every night and walk with every day. Tormented sounds like too strong a word, but that's how I feel. Something's at my guts all the time. All the time."

Beatrice didn't answer and when he heard her steady breathing, he slipped out of bed, grabbed a package of Camels and went out to the front porch steps. The lighter flared and he inhaled the scent of lighter fluid. The snap of the metal lid closing resounded in the darkness. He leaned back against the wooden post. If only he could snap his memories shut that easily.

He'd had so many plans. When the war was over he'd planned to divorce Bea and send for Heather. But now he knew he wouldn't divorce Bea, would never send for Heather. He'd lived through that bloody hell on Omaha Beach, only to go looking for Heather when the war ended and found a crater where her flat had been.

The next morning he couldn't recall how long he'd sat there staring into the black night, opening and closing the lid to his lighter, willing himself to numbness. He had deep circles under red rimmed eyes, evidence that he hadn't slept much. Beatrice was in the bathroom when he grabbed a cup of coffee and headed for his office.

Larry felt under a flowerpot for his key and when he looked up Anna Lee was standing beside him. She had a thermos and a couple of chipped coffee mugs.

"You expecting company?"

"No, sir. Just you. Thought you might like some coffee."

"I have some but it could stand warming up." Larry unlocked the door and Anna Lee followed him inside.

She put the cups and thermos on his desk and looked around. "I like the way you have all your drawings covering the walls, especially that one." She pointed to a sketch of curved, indistinct lines. "It almost looks like two people."

"It does, doesn't it? Something I never finished."

"Do the pictures help you think of ways to do scenes and maybe give people ideas of what they want to talk to you about?"

"I hope so. They help me."

"Do you get ideas when you walk in the woods?"

Larry flushed. "Lord, but you get around. How'd you know I walk in the woods?"

"I like to go out to the old cemetery sometime, and I've seen you."

"Well, don't tell anybody, okay? I just want some privacy, some time to myself."

"I haven't said anything to anybody but you."

"Let's keep it that way."

"Yes, sir." She opened the thermos and poured coffee into his cup and filled one for herself that she'd put milk and sugar in before she left home.

"How long you been drinking coffee, Anna Lee?"

"Since I was two."

"Two!"

"That's what Daddy says."

"Guess it's better than smoking."

"That's what Daddy says. Want me to straighten up some for you? I can sweep a little. It's awful dusty in here."

"I don't know, Anna Lee. I don't want you to feel like you have to come here and work. That's no way to spend your Saturday morning."

"You've given me drawing lessons so I could clean a little to pay you back."

"Okay. But just a little. I have to go outside and check on some marble samples I got last week."

She straightened some papers on Larry's desk, found a broom in a large walk-in closet and set to work. The office was overly warm so she raised one of the windows to let fresh air in and allow some dust to escape. When she was done she rinsed her cup and left it on the metal sink in the closet before going outside to find Larry. He was passing his hands over a piece of white veined marble.

Anna Lee moved her index finger along the smooth surface near Larry's hand. "I like the way it feels. Mama says you're doing a wonderful thing with your life scenes, that you're really helping people."

"I'm glad she feels that way. Thank her for me."

"No, sir, I can't do that. I don't want her to know I come here. But I think you're about the smartest man I know."

Larry smiled. "I don't know about that now . . ."

"Honest. To actually see something of a person on a tombstone. A real person. Who ever saw an angel anyway?"

"My feelings exactly."

Anna Lee kicked at a tuft of grass with the toe of her shoe. "I wish someone had done that for . . . I mean could you look at a life scene and get to know somebody you never met, even if they were dead?"

"I guess so. A little anyway. Do I hear your mother calling you?"

"Yes, sir, but, Mr. Larry, did you ever meet my real mother?"

Larry coughed. "Why, Anna Lee, I see you mother all the time. You know that."

"I mean my real mother."

"Oh, honey, we can't talk about this."

"But you're the only person I've ever told. I think everybody in town knows but me. I'm not supposed to know. I wish I had a picture—something."

Afraid she was going to cry, Larry knelt and grasped her shoulders. "Anna Lee, I can't help you there. Forget I ever admitted this, but I never knew your birth mother. I wish I had, but I didn't."

"Daddy's real, my blood kin. I overheard him and Uncle Johnn talking once."

"I don't believe I understand."

"Neither does Mama. She doesn't know it. I bet he's scared to tell her. We have more secrets than Carter has liver pills."

"I think maybe you're right, but you know what? I still hear your mama calling you. Another minute and she's liable to lose her temper."

Head bowed, she went inside and came back with her thermos.

"Don't forget your cups."

"Could I leave them here?"

Larry smiled. "That's fine. But you better go now."

"I'll run. She does sound mad."

Larry went inside and sat at his desk. *Poor kid. And they think they're doing her a favor. I wonder how long she's known. And God help everybody if Estelle Owens finds out Robert's been holding out on her. I wouldn't care to be around for that battle.*

Larry rested his head on his arms and thought of his own secret, his life scene with Heather, the one Anna Lee had singled out. Indistinct lines curving together. Heather's head thrown back exposing the curve of her throat, and her arms looped around his neck. He and Heather together for all eternity, but no one would ever guess from the vague outline he'd tacked up with the other pictures. No one would ever know. He was exhausted, and the warmth of his office made him sluggish.

There was a slight breeze from the window Anna Lee had opened. Larry closed his eyes, hoping for sleep. The last thing he wanted to do was go home. How much longer could he tolerate the guilt? Bea was the victim, and he didn't know what to do about it.

CHAPTER
Ten

June 1946

Heather stood on the sidewalk and looked around. New York City. How she'd dreamed of being here. She'd asked the cab driver to drop her off at a cheap rooming house, and she stood there looking up, dizzy with fear and anticipation. And maybe hunger. She didn't have much money, but this was a vital part of her journey. She lifted her suitcase and went inside.

Three days should do it. She could get rested and buy a couple of nice outfits. No hope of getting anything decent back home. London was a bombed out shell of itself, and goods were still scarce. She was sick of the craters, of buildings with their interiors exposing the lives of people who'd lived there. In some, family pictures still hung on the walls above piles of rubble.

But today the sun was shining, and Heather walked through neighborhoods of upright buildings, people rushing to their jobs, well dressed and amply fed. She'd had real butter on her toast that morning, the first in years, but that didn't make her feel a part of the throngs of people. She hated them. Hated them for having all the things they'd done without in England, for holding their heads high without worry of Doodlebugs, those frightening bombs that buzzed above their heads—if you were lucky. When they didn't buzz, they exploded. What had these New Yorkers given up after all? Their dead lost their lives oceans away. Their buildings remained tall and straight. Well, she intended to have a piece of their pie. Larry would help her forget the past and build a new future. She knew he would.

Bay Harbor felt worlds away from New York City. It was a long, hot, exhausting bus ride. Only thoughts of Larry cheered her. She'd relived their time together so often even the memory had begun to fray, and she tried to imagine their reunion. There were lapses though, those panicked moments, when she couldn't recall his face. Those were the times she was afraid, when she doubted the wisdom of her decision, for having fought and scraped to make this long, risky trip to America. In the end, she steeled herself with the memory of what she'd gone through during the war, of the courage it took to strike out on her own like this. There was no storm she couldn't weather. She deserved better, and she was determined to have it.

When the bus groaned to a stop in Bay Harbor, and she started down the steps, the driver grabbed her around the waist and swung her to the ground. He winked at her, and she felt things had already begun to look up. She took her suitcase into the bus station and went to the loo, changed clothes, splashed water on her face and wiped her body with a handkerchief dampened with water and a few drops of cologne she'd saved for the occasion. She rubbed toothpaste on her teeth with a finger and applied a bit of lipstick and powder.

When she emerged feeling refreshed and stylish, the woman behind the counter called out to her, "There's other women waiting to get in there too, you know." Heather looked over her shoulder and noticed a matronly woman rushing for the loo. She started to apologize but thought better of it when she saw the pinched mouth and curious eyes of the woman who'd yelled at her. She smiled and looked around the dank, unwelcoming waiting room, longing for a cup of strong, hot tea. Instead she took a deep breath and continued her journey. She walked out the door and toward what looked like the main street of town where she asked a young girl for directions to the office of Mr. Larry Rose.

Heather was flustered when the child suggested she use the taxi parked in front of the bus station.

"It's too far for you to walk with that heavy suitcase. Jimmy Tom knows the way."

"Jimmy Tom?"

"Yes'em. He's the only taxi driver we've got."

Why hadn't she thought of a taxi in the first place? She thanked the girl, and walked back to the station with as much dignity as she could muster and got in the taxi. After a brief ride, the driver, stealing glances at her in the rearview mirror, pulled over when they came to a small building behind a funeral home.

A lawyer's office? Was this what Larry meant by a small town lawyer? "Are you sure this is Mr. Rose's office?"

"Oh, yes ma'am, I'm sure. Been in there many times myself. Don't look like much compared to the funeral home, does it?"

"No, I have to say it doesn't." She'd come all this way . . . Unsettling fear gripped her. With a sinking heart she asked, "Is Mr. Rose the grounds man?"

The man laughed. "No ma'am, Mr. Larry sure ain't no grounds man."

"Oh well, no matter." She was so nervous she handed him one of her precious dollar bills without waiting for the change. He put her bag down beside a tombstone and returned to his taxi. As soon as he pulled away, she drew a deep breath and tapped on the door.

Not sleeping well at night, more and more often Larry napped at his desk. Today was no exception. He had fallen asleep, the sketch he'd been working on pushed to one side. Hearing a faint tapping like that of a child, Larry, sluggish and sleepy, called, "Anna Lee?"

The knob turned and Heather opened the door. "Were you expecting Anna Lee?"

Everything went black. Certain it was just another dream, Larry didn't even raise his head from the desk when he called, "Heather?"

"Are you surprised?"

Larry opened his eyes and struggled to his feet. Heather closed the distance between them and rushed into his arms. It was so natural, so welcome, he kissed her passionately. "My darling, oh God, my darling!" He held her at arms length trying to memorize everything about her from the stylish grey and white striped suit to the black patent leather heels that set off her trim ankles. Her hair hung just below her shoulders, like Tyler's. Tyler!

He remembered where they were and dropped his arms, taking a step back. There was a wrenching in his gut when he let her go. She started to turn away, and he grabbed her arm. "Wait, Heather, I'll explain. I have to talk to you, explain how things are."

Her face froze. "Larry," she whispered, "darling, you didn't marry, did you? I had to find you, no matter what. I never forgot the name of the town. Bay Harbor, Florida. Your home. I came straight here from the bus station. She bit her lower lip. "There isn't someone else, is there?"

"I'm married, Heather. I always was."

Her knees buckled, but he caught her elbows and kicked the door shut with his foot. "I was going to tell you. I swear, I was going to tell you. I just didn't want to spoil things between us at the time. After the war I intended to confess—everything."

"And that was going to make you a decent chap? Telling me a married man had been making love to me. I knew the reputation the G.I.'s had, but I thought you were different, Larry. I swear I thought you were different. I believed you loved me."

"Oh, Jesus," he groaned, "I did love you. I do love you. I always will. Oh, darling, don't cry." He pulled her into his arms, held her tight against his body. "You don't know what hell I've been through. I planned to get a divorce and send for you. But I hadn't figured on Normandy and being in the hospital all that time. And then when I went looking for you, your flat was nothing but a hole in the earth. No one knew where you were. I supposed you'd been killed and wanted to die myself. Went on wanting to die until two minutes ago."

"But, darling, we're together now. We can make it right, can't we?"

Larry didn't answer but held her in a fierce grip, burying his face in her hair. "I can't think right now. I'm still in shock. I thought I'd never see you again. I'm still not sure you're real."

Heather placed his hand on her left breast. "Believe me, I'm real."

For the first time since Normandy, Larry's body pulsed with life. He was covering her face and neck with kisses when he felt her body stiffen. "What's wrong?"

"I heard something," she whispered.

Larry walked over and closed the window. He lowered the shade and took Heather in his arms once more.

They stayed that way a long time, just holding each other, swaying a little, uneasy on their feet until Larry carried her to his chair, never taking his arms from her body. His lips moved against her throat. "We'll work this out, Heather. Just give me time. You have to understand I thought you were dead."

"I realize now how stupid I was to come here."

"No! Darling, this is where you belong. Here with me."

"But, Larry, I never considered you might be dead. I never thought . . . And you were in the hospital?"

"Yes, for a long time. Didn't know who I was. Lost my dog tags at Normandy. But I don't want to talk about that. Everything's okay now." He saw her looking at the drawings on the wall and said, "There is something else you need to know. I'm not practicing law any more."

"Not practicing . . ."

"No. I'm working with my brother, following my early artistic inclinations. I do life scenes for tombstones."

"Life scenes?"

He explained it to her, just as he had to Bea, wondering how she'd react.

She stared at him for a few moments and then placed her palm on the side of his face. "I love you, Larry, and I'll go on loving you no matter what. If this is important to you, then it's important to me as well. After all, you told me your family was in the funeral home business. The connection was already there."

"To hear you say that, Heather, to know you understand . . ." His voice broke, and she kissed his mouth, hard, greeting his tongue with hers in the old familiar way. His heart was pounding, and he couldn't draw a deep breath for a few moments.

"We'll work it all out, but for now let's see about getting you a place to stay. I think Helen's Boarding House would be our best bet. It's plain, but it's clean and in the heart of town. The meals are good, and they don't come any better than Helen. How are you fixed for money?"

"How expensive is the boarding house?" She looked at the floor and said, "I thought I'd be staying with you."

"Yes, and you should be, will be as soon as I can get it all worked out. Until then, you stay at Helen's. I have a place in the woods. It's nothing permanent, little more than a shack, but we can go there to have time alone, have time together while we plan our course of action." He reached in the drawer of his desk and pulled out his wallet. He began counting bills, and she pushed his hand away.

"Larry, don't do that. I'll get by on what I have. I can't take your money."

"What do you mean, you can't? Of course you can. You took all your savings to come here, didn't you?"

"Yes, but . . . I feel so cheap somehow."

"My dearest, that's the last thing I want you to feel. You're not some floozy. You're going to be my wife. I want to make this easy for you. This is only money. You've given me my life back."

"Oh, Larry, I can't tell you how wonderful it is just to see you, to touch you. Just the scent of your skin, the smell that's you. You don't know how I've dreamed of this."

"And I've thought of nothing but you and our time together. I thought that was all we'd ever have, those hours in London." He took her in his arms again, slid his hand to her buttocks and pulled her hard against him. "I've got to stop this or I'll never let you go. Tongues wag in a small town. We'll need to watch our step, be careful until I figure out how to handle this. You've never looked lovelier, but you have to be exhausted. I'll call a taxi."

"Jimmy Tom?"

He laughed. "Yes, the one and only. See, you're settling in already. Just let me hold you until he gets here, and then I'll force myself to let you go."

CHAPTER
Eleven

Saturday Evening

"You don't have to apologize to me, sugar. Eggs will be just fine."
Robert sat at the kitchen table thinking how much he hated fried eggs for supper. "Don't I know you been on your feet all day? You think I like you having to work so hard? Hell no! I wish you could sit home and crochet all day long and have somebody to fetch and carry for you."

Estelle started laughing.

"Don't laugh. Honest to God, that's how I feel. Don't you think I feel half a man sometime when I know you're over there slaving away in the drugstore till all hours. Almost makes me sick."

Anna Lee began setting the table. "Daddy, did you see a pretty woman with a big suitcase downtown today?"

"Don't know that I did. Why?"

"I thought maybe she was a war bride. She didn't talk like us."

"Could be. Never can tell what them soldiers are liable to bring home. Foreign women don't know light bread from a biscuit. Them boys have had their last good meal."

Estelle tied an apron around her waist, cinching it just a little bit more than usual, and took a bowl of cold rice out of the refrigerator. "This isn't fresh."

"Hon, I done told you. It don't matter. If it'd help you get done in the kitchen sooner I'd eat it right out of the bowl."

"No, you wouldn't. We're not heathens. We may be poor, but we've got better breeding than that."

"Yeah, sugar, but we ain't always got to be poor. They ain't no law that says we cain't better ourselves."

Estelle snorted. "Well, we're not getting rich on what you and I make. You're no Hilton Fields, you know."

"No, but I'm glad you brought that up."

"Brought what up?"

"Hilton. Me and Hilton been talking. I'll tell you about it later when you can sit down and rest some."

"You're awfully concerned about me tonight. I don't trust you when you get like this, Robert Owens. It doesn't usually spell good news for me."

"Now how can you say that, Stelle, when I'm here wanting you to get done so's you can rest?"

"I don't like anything you and Hilton cook up. I don't trust him any further than I could throw a constipated elephant."

"Now, Stelle, I don't want to hear any more of that kind of talk. There ain't nothing Hilton wouldn't do for me, if I asked him. Nothing."

"Then ask him how you can get rich too."

Lord God, she was playing right into his hands. "That's not a bad idea at all, Stelle."

Estelle snorted. "You say you're like brothers. Tell him to put some of that brotherly love in your billfold."

She was going too far, but Robert couldn't afford to lose his temper. He needed to keep her in a good mood, but it was mighty damn hard to do at times.

Robert tried to appear casual, unhurried as they ate supper at the metal-topped kitchen table. He knew Estelle would have died before she'd serve something as piss poor as eggs and rice at the dining room table.

"I'm coming home a little early tonight, Stelle. Probably before ten."

Estelle looked up and, seeing the panic in her eyes, Robert laughed. They had a set pattern for lovemaking, and this wasn't the night.

"I just want some time to talk. We never get to talk any more."

"I never realized it was so important to you."

"Well, maybe I didn't either till we didn't get to do it. You got to go out this evening?"

"I told Johnn I'd come down and help him with the books. I won't be long though."

Robert left the table and pulled on his hat, careful how he adjusted the brim. He patted his back pocket to see if he had some Prince Albert.

At ten o'clock, Robert parked the car in his front yard. He took a little box out of his shirt pocket and examined the contents in the dim light. Hell, the box was velvet. That was a gift in itself, wasn't it? Hilton hadn't thought so. He'd helped Robert choose the ring and advanced him the money to pay for it. And that was all right cause they were friends, and like Hilton said, Robert was the one doing him a favor.

Robert walked in the house patting the little box in his shirt pocket. Estelle looked up. "You got indigestion?"

"No, sugar, I was just checking to be sure I hadn't forgotten something."

"Robert, if you call me sugar one more time, I'm going to hit you in the mouth."

"Why sug . . ., I mean, Stelle, what's got into you?"

"It's nothing that's got into me, Robert Owens, and you know it. More to the point is what you're up to. It's sugar this and sugar that all night long. It's not natural."

"Well, I never knew it. You're always like sugar to me and that's the honest to God truth. You can hit me if you want to. I swear, you're the most suspicious woman ever lived."

"I just know you. You're up to something."

"Of course I am. Mainly trying to support my family."

Robert sat on the couch beside her, and she stiffened. "What's wrong?"

"You scare me, Robert. How often have you ever sat on this couch beside me? When Papa died. I remember that. Has somebody died?"

"Nobody's died, Stelle. But we got some talkin' to do. Serious talkin'."

"Yes?"

Robert wished Hilton was with him. It seemed so easy when Hilton was with him. "It's a business proposition, Stelle."

"Business? You're cozying up to me to talk business?"

"It's serious, Stelle. Not something I can do on my own. I have to have your help. Your blessing."

She stared at him. "God. Now I really am scared."

"There ain't no cause to be scared, but we have to be sure about this."

"About what? For God's sake, Robert, quit beating around the bush."

"Well, me and Hilton's been talking . . ."

"Now didn't I say it'd have something to do with Hilton!"

"Do you want me to finish or do you want to go badmouthing somebody's trying to help us out? Just listen. You know Hilton wants to settle down. Here in Bay Harbor."

"That's what he claims. I'm not sure Bay Harbor is big enough for the two of you."

"It may not have to be."

"What's that supposed to mean?"

"You know how Hilton's always had to travel so much to look after his interests and all? Well, the man he hired while he was overseas was just plain sorry. He left things in a fine mess for Hil."

"So Hilton's got a mess and wants you to be the one to clean it up?"

"You know so much. You want to tell me what I want to talk to you about?"

"I have an idea except I can't believe even Hilton would ask such a thing of a family man."

"Well, he did. Estelle, I'd be my own boss for the first time in my life."

"No, you'd be working for Hilton."

"When I'm on the road, I'll be my own man."

"I can see what's in this for him. He'd be semi-retired and free to tomcat all he wants. What's in it for you?"

"For us, Stelle. Me, you and Anna Lee."

Estelle sat speechless as Robert outlined Hilton's proposal. "And God forbid if anything should happen to Hilton in the meantime, there'd be a will naming me as a beneficiary of the property. We'd be fixed for life.

In fact, I think it's too generous, but Hil realizes it will be a strain on the family for me to be away so much of the time."

"But, Robert, we wouldn't be a family any more. What about Anna Lee? When would we see you?"

"I admit I'd be away a lot. But Hilton would be right here if anything happened. You could always call on Hilton."

"Or Johnn."

"Well, sure and Johnn too. And you wouldn't have to work any more if you don't want to. It'd be tight, but this way you'd be getting something now, not ten years down the road."

"Do you mean that? I could quit work?"

"If you want to."

"But you don't want me to, do you?"

"I want what'll make you able to handle things while I'm away."

"I'll keep working. For now. If things get rough or Anna Lee doesn't get on well, then we'll see. I might cut my hours some. I don't like it, Robert, not one little bit, but I can see the sense of it. It'll be worth the sacrifice in the long run. I hope."

"You're a good woman, Stelle. I told Hilton you were a trooper. And I saved the best part till last. I know what store you alus set on Miz Field's house. Well, Hilton said if we'd rather, instead of two hundred acres, he'd deed me a hundred and Miz Field's house when she passes. I figured you'd like that house."

Estelle sat open-mouthed. Robert was afraid she might be having a stroke until she said, "To live in that house! It's even nicer than Amy and Johnn's place. Why would he do that?"

"Hilton's never wanted to live there, but he knows it's a showpiece. He'd like to keep it in the family so to speak, with us in it. There's only one catch though."

She rolled her eyes. "Here it comes."

"That part of the deal is just between us. He don't want his mother thinking he's planning for her to die. Fact is, I'd like to keep the entire deal between us. No use in the whole town knowing our business."

"I agree." Estelle started to cry. "Oh, Robert, it's like a fairytale."

Robert grabbed her to him in an awkward embrace.

"Ouch! What in the world have you got in your pocket?"

"Lord help. I almost forgot." Robert fished the little box out of his shirt pocket. He looked at it a moment, running his thumb back and forth over the velvet lid.

"This isn't a joke is it, Robert? You've never been one for gifts in velvet boxes. A box of guava jelly maybe or an ugly green frog doorstop. But a velvet box?"

"I wish I could of gotten you this for nothing. I mean, for no special reason. Maybe in ten years I can give you presents for no occasion. This is to remind you why I'm away and what we got to look forward to." He handed her the box and she stared at it a minute before she lifted the lid.

"Oh! It takes my breath away. It's beautiful. Just beautiful." The green topaz winked at her from its gold filigree mounting. "I am sorry you're going on the road, and I will miss you terribly, but, Robert, this ring makes up for a lot. An awful lot."

Robert silently congratulated himself and wondered just how far he could stretch her gratitude.

CHAPTER
Twelve

Anna Lee didn't know what she should wear to Lola's party. After all, she was only helping serve and didn't want Lola to laugh at her if she wore a Sunday dress. She spent a lot of time looking through her clothes before deciding on a white peasant blouse and gathered skirt of black and white checks that made her look a little less skinny.

Afraid Lola wouldn't let her help with the party if she knew, Anna Lee hadn't let on Hilton wouldn't be driving her there. She walked to the lighthouse instead and ignored the forced smile on Lola's face when she answered the door looking radiant in her new birthday dress.

"I thought Hilton . . ."

"Mama wouldn't let me ask him."

Without a word Lola turned on her heel and walked into the living room that had been decorated for the party.

Anna Lee looked up at the balloons hung from the ceiling and at the pale green and white crepe paper swaged over the windows.

"The paper matches my dress and my birthstone," Lola said, flashing the heart-shaped pearl ring her parents had given her early, before Captain Edwards left town on business. "And see, my dress is nearly the same color as the punch."

Anna Lee looked in the punch bowl and could see she was right. Lola's organdy dress was a pale lime green that accented her long auburn hair. "If you spill punch on your dress, it'll never show."

Lola's nose flared slightly. "I don't spill things on my clothes, thank you, and that isn't why it matches the punch. Anna Lee, you have no imagination, none whatever."

When her friends began arriving Lola started some records on the phonograph. Anna Lee asked her to play *Mairzy Doats*, but Lola placed the needle in the groove of *Give Me Something To Remember You By*. Anna Lee and Virginia sat at the breakfast nook in the kitchen and listened to the laughter from the front room. Bing Crosby sang *Moonlight Becomes You* and Anna Lee knew Lola and her friends were slow dancing again.

After she'd helped serve refreshments, Anna Lee and Virginia returned to their seats in the breakfast nook. Anna Lee looked at some of the left-over petit fours and said, "I could fit a whole one of those in my mouth."

"So could I," Virginia answered. "Shall we?" Laughing they popped green petites fours into their mouths. Their cheeks were bulging with cake when they heard someone knocking on the front door. Virginia's eyes grew wide and she spit the cake into a napkin.

The revelers grew quiet in the front room, and Virginia composed herself and opened the swinging door that separated the kitchen from the front room.

Hilton stood at the front door. He smiled, gave a mock bow, and then looked at Anna Lee. "Your mother asked if I'd give you a ride home." Anna Lee started toward Hilton, but he looked at Virginia and asked, "May I have a dance with the birthday girl first?"

Anna Lee thought Virginia was going to cry, but she just nodded and Lola selected a new record. She glided into Hilton's arms as Frank Sinatra crooned *Night and Day*. When the song ended, Hilton motioned to Anna Lee to come with him.

"Hilton, just a minute," Virginia called. "Before you take Anna Lee home could you give me a ride to the store? We need some more ginger ale."

Hilton's eyes twinkled. "I'm not sure anything will be open, Mrs. Edwards. We might have to drive a ways to find ginger ale this time of night."

"Well, this is the only sixteenth birthday party Lola will ever have so I'm willing to make the effort. Anna Lee, I'm leaving you in charge. Keep an eye on these young people while I'm gone. No funny business now, you hear?"

Just as Hilton had predicted, there wasn't a store open in town. Every place they passed was dark. "I'll drive out a little farther and see if we can find anything open, but I doubt there will be."

"Do you have any cigarettes?" Virginia kept pulling her wedding band off and on her finger.

Hilton glanced her way. "I wouldn't have figured you for a smoker."

She tucked one leg under her and turned to face him. "I don't smoke, but I want a cigarette."

"If you say so. I could offer you my pipe, but check the glove compartment. Might be some in there."

Virginia rummaged around and found a flattened package of Lucky Strike. "Some of your lady friends smoke?" She worked a cigarette from the pack and Hilton pushed the lighter in to heat.

"What makes you think I have lady friends?"

"Didn't you just say you smoke a pipe? But don't play coy with me, Mr. Fields. I know you better than you think."

"Is that so?" He touched the glowing lighter to her cigarette.

"Oh, yes. That's so. You don't remember me, do you?" She smoothed her skirt over her legs, keeping her head lowered.

"Remember you from what?"

She looked up, flipping her blue-black hair with the back of her left hand. "Does Hedy Lamarr ring a bell?"

"Hedy Lamarr?"

She let out a heavy sigh of disappointment. "You were so young. I guess I shouldn't be insulted. Many years ago I was visiting my uncle in Tallahassee, and you and I happened to be at the same banquet. I've never forgotten all those magnolia leaves they sprayed gold and used to decorate the table. I stared at them to keep from looking at you, but luck was on my side. My uncle became ill and had to leave early. They asked you to give me a ride home. Remember now?"

Hilton gave a low whistle. "That was you?"

She tilted her head back and blew smoke through pursed lips. "Oh yes. Only I never forgot you. And it wasn't just your hair that made me remember." She reached out, pressing a forefinger just above his temple.

"God. That was you? I can't believe it!"

"Don't insult me. Surely I haven't changed that much!"

"It isn't that. It was such a long time ago."

"A very long time, but I'm not saying anything, and I don't want you to either. I was in a troubled marriage, and you were sweet and gallant to an older woman."

"A very pretty woman, and not all that old, I recall. More like a child bride, I'd say."

"I was lonely and frustrated."

"If you're still in a troubled marriage, I'll be glad to oblige you again." Hilton laughed, seeming to make a joke of his offer.

"Oh, I'm sure you would. My marriage isn't perfect, but whose is? We both love Lola. She's helped a lot."

"She's lovely. You have every right to be proud of her."

"Yes, she is lovely, and she has a crush on you. I'm warning you though, stay away from her. I don't want her winding up in the back seat of your car. Ever!"

"Yes ma'am." He knew he was a fool to toy with this woman, but couldn't seem to help himself. "I'll keep that reserved for her mother."

Virginia laughed. "You just do that, you hear?"

Hilton parked the car under a towering oak at the side of a darkened store. "I'm not joking," he said and went around and hesitated only a moment before he opened Virginia's door.

"I can't do this, Hilton. I have a reputation, and Lola . . ." She got out of the car and pressed her body to his.

They got in the back seat and he pushed her down, covering her body with his. "I'm beginning to remember. It's all coming back."

Virginia laughed. "I can tell."

Hilton pushed her to the edge of the seat and lay on his side facing her. She put her face close to his and laid her hand on his cheek. "You were such a boy, such a horny boy."

When he cupped her left breast, he felt her nipple harden against his palm.

"You haven't changed a bit."

"You haven't either, Mrs. Edwards."

"Except that I have a daughter now. Oh, Hilton . . ." She swallowed hard. "We can't do this. I can't go back to that party looking like I've been laid."

"What a pity." He sat up and got out of the car. *What am I doing? I live here now!*

Virginia stepped out of the car and smoothed her dress. "Let me have your handkerchief." She wiped the smeared lipstick from her mouth and then used slow, even strokes to clean smudges from his lips. "I have the excuse of having consumed an entire petite four. You're on your own for yours." She folded the handkerchief and handed it to him.

"I'm not a young boy any more. I believe I can handle it."

She shot back, "See that you do, especially in front of my daughter. We're not going to find any ginger ale tonight. Let's go back. I don't want to be accused of not chaperoning Lola's party. I just had to get that off my chest, to let you know we'd met before."

"And a lovely chest it is too."

"You really haven't changed."

"You wouldn't want me to."

"Maybe not." She reached inside the car, crushed her cigarette in the ashtray and slammed it shut. "Remember, no one is to know we've met before."

"I'm not here to make trouble for anybody."

"Good. Neither am I."

Anna Lee leaned out the window and waved good-by to Lola. Hilton eased the car onto the highway. "Did you enjoy the party?"

She gave a harsh laugh. "No chance of that. I wasn't even invited. I was there to help Mrs. Edwards serve." Anna Lee slipped out of her shoes and propped her feet on the dashboard.

"I guess you're a little young for Lola's friends."

"That's what Lola said, but I might've embarrassed her too."

"Now, you don't think that."

"Sure I do. I'm not as proper as Lola. She'd never put her feet up like this. I haven't even figured out what to do with an olive pit."

Hilton glanced at her. "An olive pit?"

"You know, if you're at a fancy dinner. Where would you put it?"

Hilton laughed. "You've got me there. Guess it's a good thing I wasn't invited to the party either."

"Lola's pretty, isn't she?"

"Sure is. Pretty as a speckled pup under a red wagon in the sunshine. That was one of my dad's favorite sayings."

"I like sayings. That would have to be pretty, all right. Some girls have all the luck—looks and everything."

"Wait till you grow up, Anna Lee. You'll be a knockout."

"Just cause you're Daddy's best friend, you don't have to say that."

"But I mean it. Just you wait."

"I've been waiting all my life."

"That hasn't been all that long, you know. One of these days you'll wake up and the wait'll be over."

"I hope so, but Mama says on top of everything else I'm getting a bad temper."

"Puberty."

"No, Mama says it's temper. Says I'm downright mean any more."

"We're all mean sometimes, even mamas."

"You can see me telling her that, can't you?"

Hilton laughed. "Maybe you better not. There's an African proverb that says, 'All truth is good, but not all truth is good to say.'"

"Now that's a really good saying. I'm going to write it down. There's lots of things I wouldn't dare say to Mama, not if I didn't want a switching."

"Surely you're too old . . ."

"I don't think I'll ever be too old for switching. No matter how much I want to, there are just things I can't say even if they are true."

"You're a smart girl, Anna Lee. Be your own counsel. You got any friends your own age, girls who'd invite you to their parties?"

"Maybe one or two. My best friend was Mark, but he moved away."

"So you had a boyfriend, huh?"

"No, but I liked him a lot. I don't want a boyfriend. I'd rather hear about Tyler and Lola's boyfriends. They're more interesting."

"That'll change soon. Boys your own age will become more interesting to you."

"I can't imagine that."

"You'll be surprised what you'll be able to imagine one of these days."

Hilton stopped the car in front of the Owens' house and reached over to open her door. "Night, beautiful."

Anna Lee stifled a small gasp and walked around to the other side of the car. "I'm glad you're Daddy's best friend." She started toward the house and looked back. "And not because of what you just said."

After he let Anna Lee off, Hilton reached in the glove compartment for the Lucky Strikes and realized Virginia had let them fall on the floor. It annoyed him that she hadn't put them back where they belonged. But then, what could you expect from a married woman who slept around on her husband?

He remembered her all right. Down through the years he called up the memory. Sexually deprived, that's what she'd been, only he was too young to recognize it at the time. The memory stirred him in ways he didn't like, kindled desires he couldn't satisfy. He felt restless and uncomfortable. He lit a cigarette and backed the car onto the road.

He inched along the street, slowing even more as he drove past the funeral home. He saw a blur of white and realized the Rose girl had just walked down her front steps. He tooted the horn quietly and she waved. He drove past her house, inhaled deeply on his cigarette, and turned the car around. Tyler sat on the porch steps hugging her knees.

"You look lonely", he called. "Want to go for a spin?"

"Thanks. Yeah, I would. I'll tell my mother and be right out."

What in God's name was he doing? She was just a kid. Damn that

Edwards woman for stirring up memories. Back then, Hilton recalled, *he'd* been the kid.

Tyler took her time getting back outside. She finally emerged from the house looking cool and collected. "You're out late tonight, Mr. Fields."

"I could say the same for you, Miss Rose."

"Yes, but this is my home. I spend many late evenings on my front porch."

"Well, Bay Harbor is my home now too. You're liable to see me most any time of the day or night."

"Is that so?"

"Absolutely."

Tyler betrayed her nervousness when, sounding as though it was as unusual as a shooting star, she said, "Look! Heat lightning!" The dark sky brightened with an explosion of distant light.

"There's no such thing as heat lightning. You're just seeing someone else's storm, that's all."

"Then we see other people's storms a lot."

"Yes, we do. And when it storms in Bay Harbor, some place else a pretty girl is saying, 'Oh, look at the heat lightning.'"

"You make it sound like somewhere, somebody is missing out on something, a witness to events some place else."

"That about sums it up."

"Well it makes me sad."

"Why's that?"

"There's always been something so special about heat lightning. Like the echo of my day, the rainbow of a hot afternoon. And now you're telling me there's no such thing."

"Lord, Tyler, you make me feel like I just told you there wasn't any Santa Claus. If you went out on a winter night and saw lightning in the distance, what would you think?"

"That it was storming some place."

"And you'd be right. It's the same thing if you see distant lightning on a hot night. It's all here with you," he said and touched his finger to his forehead. "You've been perceiving something that didn't exist."

"Sometimes I think my whole world is turned upside down. There's nothing I can count on any more. Just change. That's all there is."

"Keeps you from being bored." Hilton picked up his pipe and chewed on the cold stem.

"Don't count on it." Tyler lifted her body slightly and smoothed the back of her dress, letting out a bored sigh.

Hilton dimmed the lights for a passing car. "I learned a long time ago not to count on anything."

"You have all the answers, don't you? I wish I had your ... your ..."

"My what?""

"Oh, I don't know. You just seem so satisfied, so content."

"I am. Sorry if that offends you."

"It doesn't offend me. You always take what I say the wrong way."

"I don't mean to. I enjoy your company. Wish you'd enjoy mine."

"I do. But you burst my bubble every now and then."

"You have an unusual name. Tyler."

"I know. Sounds more like a man's name. It was my grandmother's maiden name. She died before I was born, and my mother wanted to honor her."

"That's nice. Kind of sets you apart. I've never known another Tyler."

She laughed. "You probably never will,"

"How old are you anyway, Miss Rose?"

"Does it matter?"

"No, it doesn't. I'm just curious. You seem older somehow than I think you really are."

"Well then, let's leave it at that. I'm old enough to have been engaged, to have lost someone I loved in the war."

"I'm sorry to hear that."

"You mean you hadn't heard already? That's a pity. Guess I'm not the talk of the town any more."

"Not in my circle of friends anyway. Wish I could stop and buy you something to drink, but everything's closed. I found that out earlier when Mrs. Edwards tried to find more ginger ale for her daughter's birthday party."

"Mrs. Edwards?"

"I gave her a ride when I went to get Anna Lee from Lola's party. Would you be old enough to drink if I found something— something hard?"

"I'm old enough to know I don't want to drink around you."

"Okay, I give up. I have ways of finding out how old you are."

"Is it really that important to you?"

His clipped words cut through her lighthearted mood. "As a matter of fact, no. It really doesn't matter."

"Bastard," Tyler said under her breath.

"I love seeing moonlight on the water. How bout you, Miss Rose?"

"Who couldn't like moonlight?" she answered stiffly.

"Soldiers in battle."

She sighed. "Everything comes back to the war, doesn't it?"

"War isn't something you forget." He pulled the car into the park facing the pier and killed the ignition. "I hear your dad was shot up pretty bad."

"Yes."

"War's a terrible thing. I was lucky. You don't mind if I park here, do you? We can look at the moonlight on the Bay."

"Suit yourself." She sat rigid, staring straight ahead.

"Come off it. I just don't like it when women get to thinking they're so damn special. Your age is of no real consequence to me."

"You're a conceited bastard, you know that?"

"Wow! Didn't know you had it in you."

"I assure you I'm old enough to curse."

"Touché. I really am sorry about your fiancé though. That has to be tough."

"It was for awhile, but I'm getting over it. I won't ever let myself be hurt that way again."

"Never say never."

"I don't think it would be possible to hurt in just the same way. I mean, you'd never love two people the same, would you?"

"I don't know. I've never been in love, not romantically anyway."

"Are you serious?"

"Scout's honor."

"How sad."

"Nothing sad about it. I didn't say I hadn't had women. I've had my share. I've just never met one I really trusted, that I wanted to settle down with."

"Gosh," she said sarcastically. "What kind of women do you go out with?"

"All kinds." He laughed. "All kinds. But let's don't talk about other people. Let's enjoy the moonlight." He reached for her hand and held it between both of his, stroking her palm with his fingertips. "Your hands are so slender and soft."

"The kind of hands Scarlett wanted to have."

"Who?"

"You know, Scarlett in *Gone With the Wind.*"

"I guess any woman would like soft hands."

"Yours are soft too, you know."

"Are they? That's because I've been a man of leisure lately." He slid his fingers under the sleeve of her blouse, up her arm and back down across her hand.

He felt her body stiffen. "Relax, Miss Rose. I don't bite. I just love the feel of a woman."

"I thought all men did."

"Not all of 'em. Most men never take the time to really know a woman's body. It's an art, you know. Making love is an art if you do it right."

She swallowed hard. "I . . . I wouldn't know."

"But you said you'd been engaged."

"Yes, I was engaged, but Stephen respected me. He would never, I mean . . ."

"He died without, without . . .?"

Tears splashed onto Hilton's hand. "Yes, he died without. Don't think I haven't thought of that. He never pushed me though, never suggested . . ."

Hilton took her in his arms and stroked her hair. "Poor boy," he said. "Poor boy."

CHAPTER
Thirteen

Monday

Bay Harbor languished without purpose, didn't know quite how to act without a war. Despite all the fears and sacrifices, the war had given the town hope of change, of progress on the horizon, even a boom. Visions of rising real estate values, new businesses, and elegant restaurants fueled hopes for the future. There were changes, of course. Women quit driving taxis, keeping books at the bank, and working in the mills. They went home to allowances set by their husbands, to the monotony of housework, PTA, and the welcome realization that sugar and coffee were no longer luxuries.

They brought children up in new homes that were small and identical in design. There were no frills, no porches or garages and limited space for lawns or flowers. Only the color of the paint relieved the monotony. If they were lucky, their husbands went to college on the GI Bill. Things weren't exactly the way they had been before the war, yet somehow the spark of prosperity seemed to elude Bay Harbor.

The picture show's glistening billboards dulled, the paint began to fade and flake, and its dark interior became a shrine to the remembered echoes of patriotic music and visions of World War II's handsome soldiers. The picture show was no longer an escape from the reality of war. It was the reality. Life became routine again, relieved only by gossip and innuendo.

Anna Lee had no intention of adding to the gossip. She hadn't told anyone that she'd seen Larry Rose kissing Heather Rushby. She knew her name now. Estelle's hours had been cut, and they'd hired Heather part-time at the drugstore. She rented a room at Helen's boarding house, and everybody called her Heather, even children. She didn't know Southern customs and insisted Mrs. Rushby was too formal, made her feel old.

Anna Lee knew Heather had to have some place to live, but she wished it had been any place but the boarding house. Helen was her mother's best friend, but going there to visit Helen, even when Heather was at work, Anna Lee could never forget it was Heather's home now. Helen mentioned her often. She and Heather had a common bond, both having lost men they loved during the war. It gave Heather a special standing with the other boarders.

Everybody liked Heather. She did more to revive Bay Harbor than anything since the war. Heather gave people something to talk about, gave them the feeling of broadening their horizons all the way to England. But no one could understand why a young woman would come all the way from England to the United States and settle in Bay Harbor. Miami, San Francisco, Chicago, Boston, New York. Those were the places that beckoned, not Bay Harbor. Her name was on every tongue, but no one seemed able to solve the riddle. Finally Virginia Edwards asked her outright, "Why here? Why Bay Harbor?"

She was pretty and sweet, and her accent served only to . . . well, accent her charm. "Bay Harbor? Why, I just happened on it as it were, looking at the map. I liked the sound of it, you know. It sounded like magic to me, and I needed to get away. First I lost my husband and then my mum was killed when a bomb hit just as she was running for the air raid shelter. It was a small coastal town, much like Bay Harbor, and I couldn't go back there after the war, not with my mum dead. I thought Bay Harbor would just suit me.

"You've not seen London's devastation, weren't there during the war, don't know what it was like living through the air raids, not just having family and friends killed, but watching them die. Seeing homes bombed, losing your husband, losing . . . But how I go on. I was able to get away, so

I did. You don't mind my being here now, do you?"

Of course everybody wanted her there so people finally quit inquiring and absorbed her and her accent into the fabric of Bay Harbor.

Anna Lee didn't dare say anything against Heather, not when people seemed so fascinated with her. Heather could do something as rude as putting lipstick on in public, and nobody thought anything of it. Maybe that's what people did in England. But Anna Lee had felt uneasy around Larry since the day he'd nearly caught her spying on them at the open window of his office. What if he *had* seen her?

School was out, and the long summer stretched before her. She was bored and missed spending time with Larry while he sketched scenes for tombstones. Every night she asked God to help her be a better person, to help her like Heather. If everybody else liked her, why couldn't she?

Anna Lee remembered hearing the Baptist minister criticize the ladies of the Missionary Society when they wanted to make cushions for the church pews. "You don't go to God's house to be comfortable," he told them. "God went to the cross for you. Surely you can sit on a wooden bench for a few hours."

Desperate in her need, Anna Lee knelt on the hard floor by her bed, folded her hands like a small child, and pleaded with God to tell her why a married man would kiss Heather. Her knees still ached when He answered her prayer. *Of course! She only imagined Mr. Larry was kissing Heather. She had gone there on business, and he was trying to comfort her. Wouldn't it be just like Mr. Larry to do something like that!*

Convinced God had solved the problem, her spirits lifted, and the next afternoon she went straight to the funeral home. T. J. was outside trying to pump up the tires on a bicycle.

"Is that yours?"

"Birthday present. It's called a victory bike. See the skinny tires. Some present. It came with flat tires."

"Wish I had a bike. I wouldn't care if the tires were flat."

"Well, I care. It's a goddamn present."

"I guess. Still, the tires won't always be flat."

"They sure as hell won't." T. J. threw the bicycle pump aside. "Here I go. Watch me."

T. J. took off and Anna Lee watched him ride away the same way he walked, hunched over and moving his legs as fast as they'd go. He hadn't gone far when he held up his right hand and extended a crooked pinky finger in her direction. She repeated the gesture, then continued around back and tapped on Larry's door. She heard voices before he called, "It's open."

Anna Lee's heart sank. She could feel the blood drain from her face as she stood in the doorway, unsure what to do, unable to understand why she felt so uncomfortable.

Heather sat in a chair across from Larry's desk, the same chair Anna Lee had dusted several weeks earlier. Heather's face had that washed-out look people get when they're sick, and she tapped a cigarette on a package of Chesterfields. Larry stood up. "Did you want something, Anna Lee?"

She tried to say she wanted, to ask if he had time for a drawing lesson but all she could do was stammer, "I . . . I . ." She looked at Larry and back at Heather and blurted the only thing that came into her mind. "Mama says Heather took a job at the Florida Power Company."

"That's right I did."

Anna Lee continued standing in the door wondering if she should offer to sweep for Larry. She begged God to give her a reason for being there.

Larry cleared his throat. "Mrs. Rushby just stopped by to . . ." Larry looked at Heather.

"I have business with Mr. Rose. It'd be best if you left now, Anna Lee. I need to make arrangements for the burial of my baby daughter's ashes."

"A baby . . . I'm sorry." Anna Lee looked at Larry. He was deathly pale too, but she supposed a baby's ashes could do that. She smelled sulfur as Heather struck a match to light her cigarette. No one said anything as Anna Lee turned and ran out the door. Later she realized Heather had looked so white because she didn't have on any lipstick. Even though she had promised God she'd be a better person, she couldn't help but wonder if they'd been kissing again.

Larry stared at Heather, unable to speak. It bothered him that she could lie so smoothly. He knew she did it for him, but it made her seem less perfect somehow.

"You didn't have to lie to protect me, Heather."

"I didn't."

"You didn't lie? I . . ."

"We had a child, Larry. A baby girl. She was in the flat with a neighbor when the bomb hit. But I did lie. There are no ashes. She was so tiny, and there was nothing but dust and rubble . . ." She began to cry, and Larry went around the desk and knelt at her feet, burying his face in her lap. When he looked up, he couldn't control the tears. "My dearest darling. I had no idea. Of all the dreams I had of you, this was never one of them."

"Oh, Larry, I've wanted to tell you ever since I arrived, but I just couldn't. I couldn't say it . . . Darling, whatever are we going to do? I just had to be with you. I came as soon as I got enough money together. You were all I had left of . . ."

"What did you name her?"

"I didn't. I was waiting for you so we could choose a name together. She was Baby Rose on the birth certificate. I refused to give her a name without you."

"Baby Rose." Larry couldn't help himself. Already he was envisioning the rose on a tombstone. Pink marble, petals at the top. . .

"I met your daughter, Larry."

"Tyler? You met Tyler?"

"In the drugstore. Tyler Rose." Heather drew on her cigarette, tilted her head back and blue smoke hung on the air. "Such a beautiful name. A lovely young woman. At least you still have a daughter."

"Heather, don't. Let's not talk about my family. I'd give anything to undo all this for you. I love you in a way I've never loved anything or anybody, but I can't just walk in the house tonight and announce that we were lovers during the war. You've got to give me time to work things out."

"I don't seem to have a lot of choice, do I?"

"It's been such a shock to me, Heather. I hadn't begun to finish mourning you or the war when you walked in my door that afternoon. That changed everything, and now I have to devise a way of handling it with the least hurt to everyone. I don't mean to make excuses, but don't forget I was in the hospital a long time. I didn't expect to live. I did, but things don't come as easy to me as they once did."

"I know, Darling, I know. I'm sorry for being selfish, for wanting you so much."

"You owe me no apologies, Heather. It's my fault, all of it. From the start, I loved you so. I was the one being selfish. But understand, that as much as small towns possess charm and a measure of security, there is also a certain tyranny. Things are magnified in small places, not easily forgotten. I have to handle this is such a way that we will be accepted, that we can have a happy life here together. Just give me time. Please."

Okay, Larry. I'll leave it all up to you."

When she left, Larry closed the door as quietly as if a baby had been sleeping. He walked to his desk, numb with guilt. First Bea and now Heather. All Heather had been through, and he hadn't been there to help her. A daughter. Their child. How had she stood the pain?

Foster came in later and found Larry at his desk sobbing. "Sweet Jesus, Larry, what's happened?"

"Mrs. Rushby was here, Foster. She has some ashes she wants interred. She lost a baby girl in one of the bombings. It just . . . it brought all the horror of the war back."

Foster squeezed his shoulder. "You can't do a life scene for an infant anyway."

"I guess not. But I was thinking maybe I could do something in pink marble. A rose maybe . . ."

Prosperity may have eluded everyone else, but it was a gift laid at the doorstep of Robert Owens. He thought he might be the happiest man on the face of the earth. He still had trouble believing that he stood to inherit property some day. It was hard not to count the months until that day came. To be a land holder. His own man. It was nothing short of a miracle.

And he loved his new job. He whistled and hummed all day long. He was his own boss. Even people in Bay Harbor seemed to regard him with more respect, to realize he was somebody, not that he'd been any slouch as deputy sheriff. Once Robert understood what he was to do, Hilton left him in charge.

He'd never been jealous of Hilton's money, but now, with his own freedom, Robert realized how money allowed Hilton to be what he was. Not everybody knew Hil like he did. People thought he was kind of cocky at times, but Robert knew the dark doubts Hilton hid deep inside. Hilton was more vulnerable than anyone realized, more alone than he ever wanted to be.

Driving along the highway between calls, Robert thought of property Hilton could buy in Bay Harbor, the kind of house he'd build, but he could never quite imagine the kind of woman Hil would marry. That worried him. What if Hil couldn't imagine her either?

Robert slowed the car when he came to a city limits sign. The miles were adding up, and Hilton said they should look into giving Robert a company car. He'd like that. Writing on the side of a car made things more official. And then, too, he'd have a car to leave home for Stelle. Johnn let her use his car from time to time, but Robert didn't want to be beholden.

He'd gotten into a routine now. Stayed at the same boarding houses, gassed up at the same filling stations. People knew him by name in any number of towns in Georgia, Alabama, and South Carolina. And they liked him. He knew that. Was pretty sure he could have had a little fun on the side if he wanted to.

It bothered him at first that he began to feel single as soon as he saw the city limits sign of Bay Harbor in the rear- view mirror, when the salt breeze gave way to the sweet smell of corn fields, freshly turned earth or bales of hay. He thought he'd get used to it, get over it, but the feeling of being young and free grew stronger. He realized the possibilities travel afforded him. Robert Owens was a soldier in a foreign country. And even without a uniform, he knew he wasn't bad looking. Just over five feet ten inches, he knew his slender frame made him look taller, and his face was strong, large for his body, and easy to look at.

His favorite stopping place was a boarding house in South Carolina run by a widow named Emaline. He couldn't name exactly what it was, but something about her reminded him of Grace, Anna Lee's real mother.

The first time he'd seen Grace she was on the steps of a rural school-house on the outskirts of Tallahassee urging her pupils to form a straight line. Each fall he waited to see if there'd be any new teachers, and Grace didn't disappoint him. Only once would she do that. He'd pulled his car to the side of the road and stopped.

Her dark hair was cut close to her head, and her features were small, doll-like. After the students filed past her into the building, she turned and blew him a kiss, knew he'd been watching. She was saucy that way but kind too, gentle and soft spoken.

Without a word to anyone, already in love, he invited her to a dance on Saturday night. He'd held her in his arms for only two dances when his twin brother, Earl, came in the door. Robert introduced them and watched Earl fall in love too. Robert's first love would become his twin brother's wife.

All those years ago, and a part of him still loved her. Emaline was the first woman to remind him of her. *Ah, Grace*. It still hurt.

Emaline called him Mr. Owens, never anything so familiar as Robert. The other boarders called her Mrs. Howell, but to him she was just Emaline. He loved saying her name, hearing it hang on the warm, moist air.

"Emaline, could I have another slice of that chocolate pie? Best chocolate pie I ever et." He liked to think she prepared special pies and cakes when he stayed there, made them just for him.

"Better watch your figure, Mr. Owens."

She was saucy like Grace. He liked that. "You watch it for me, Emaline." He thought he saw her wink at him, something Grace would have done.

After Grace died he and Estelle left Tallahassee and moved to Bay Harbor. He thought it would quit hurting. It didn't. And there'd always be Anna Lee to remind him.

Trying to dislodge the memories, Robert thought of Emaline, her willowy body, the dark hair wound in a braid around her head.

The first time he stopped at her boarding house he felt the sweet chemistry, that palpable spark between them, but there was something so pure and kind about her that so far he'd been able to keep his desires in check. He knew he shouldn't stay there any more, that he should find another boarding house, but he couldn't help himself.

Emaline was always so neat and clean, as though she'd just come from her bath. He liked to think of how her skin would smell, the taste of it on his tongue. He swallowed hard and fought to control such musings. She was refined, subdued, and soft spoken. He never heard her raise her voice.

He wished there were something he could do for her, help her out a bit without seeming forward. He had a gold bracelet in the car. The saleslady called it a bangle. It was a smooth circlet of gold with a pattern of tiny flowers and leaves. The lady said it was the latest thing. He bought it before he had time to regret not asking Hilton to help him pick it out. It was simple enough to suit Emaline and had enough shine to suit Estelle. He wasn't sure who it was for.

He prided himself on his appearance and sensed that Emaline looked up to him. Didn't she always call him Mr. Owens? He always wore a tie, his khakis were unsoiled, and his pants bore a sharp knife pleat. He had to hand it to Estelle. She knew her way around an ironing board.

Robert Owens wasn't a peddler. Nobody avoided him for fear he'd try to sell them something. No, Hil had given him a charmed life. Surely he could give Emaline a bracelet without offending her. Maybe. Maybe not. For now he had to content himself with looking at Emaline, for being grateful to sleep under the same roof she did.

And if life wasn't exactly charmed for Stelle—well, it would be eventually. Stelle was Grace's opposite. In the beginning, when he married her, he thought that was a good thing, less hurtful, less of a reminder. She didn't give him much time to think about Grace. He stayed too busy trying to keep her temper in check. That temperament was great in bed, but the rest of the time it was a cross to bear. Maybe it was time he followed that ring up with a gold bracelet. The latest thing.

Had Robert known just how dissatisfied his wife was at that moment, there would have been no doubt in his mind about which woman should get the bracelet.

Estelle was the victim of restless nights. She lay on the bed in the dark smoking her third cigarette, wearing the only satin slip she owned. She imagined herself thinner and better looking than her mirror revealed. It was warm and all the windows were open. Every now and then a breeze rippled across her body. Estelle wasn't immune to the glamour of movies about reckless women. She traced the slip with her finger, loving its soft, sexy feel. She could have put her gown on but enjoyed the slight feeling of decadence the slip and cigarettes gave her. She avoided touching her skin. It lacked the sheen and firmness of youth, something she'd be denied for the rest of her life.

Robert hadn't even noticed she'd started smoking again. Served him right for being gone all the time. Estelle felt she was at a crossroads in her life. She was irritable and dissatisfied. Though grateful for the financial security Hilton had given them, she was restless with Robert away so much.

Some weekends when he got home, he was so tired he never even thought of sex. At first Estelle figured that was pretty normal for a man Robert's age. Then she began to worry. What if he'd met someone? Weren't boarding houses always run by beautiful widows? Could Robert have met a young widow who ran one where he stayed?

The problem was, the more she thought about Robert and any new love interest he might have, the more attractive he became. It excited her to think other women might find him appealing. She imagined him with someone else and her body warmed to the thought. She began competing for his attention. Weekends when he came home she could hardly wait to go through his clothes searching for some tell-tale sign of a dalliance, a bit of lipstick, a long strand of red hair, a note, a receipt. Anything.

CHAPTER
Fourteen

July 1946

A summer storm smudged black across a pale blue sky. Dark clouds chewed at the sunlight and the house grew dark. Anna Lee closed windows and turned on several lights, but a sense of unease she couldn't name fell over her like a cloud from the storm. She grabbed the raincoat Lola had given her and headed for the lighthouse. The blowing sand stung, but she walked along the beach. Her dad had forbidden her to use the highway. He had seen too many drunks racing down the beach road when he was sheriff.

Anna Lee climbed the steps and thrilled to the howling wind that rattled the lighthouse windows. She heard music and could just make out *I Couldn't Sleep a Wink Last Night*. Through the tall narrow windows by the door she watched Virginia swaying, hugging herself as she danced. Anna Lee knocked several times before Virginia took the record off the phonograph and came to the door.

"Well, look what the wind blew in. Come inside. The bottom will drop out any minute now." She made no explanation for her disheveled hair or the fact that she'd been dancing.

The house smelled like salt air and freshly brewed coffee. "How'd you like some coffee? I was just about to pour myself a cup."

"Yes ma'am, I'd like some." She looked around. "Is Lola here?"

"She went to the show, something with Judy Garland, I believe. She should be back any time now, but I'm afraid she's going to be soaked." Virginia put a heavy yellow cup and saucer in front of Anna Lee. "You take milk and sugar, don't you?"

"Yes, ma'am. I wish I could drink it black the way Lola does, but it tastes like wet cigarette ashes."

"Well, it took her a long time, but she was determined she'd be drinking black coffee when she went to college."

"Why?"

"She thinks college girls wear plaid skirts and drink black coffee all day. Maybe they do, for all I know."

"I won't go to college then. I don't think I'll ever drink it black."

"Don't try it all at once, Anna Lee. Most things are conquered a little at the time. Just work up to it gradually, reducing the milk and sugar slightly with every cup. That's how Lola did it, and now she says it makes her sick to even imagine it any other way."

"I didn't know Lola was so interested in college."

"We've discussed it a lot lately. Darrell and I are considering sending her away to prep school. Maybe as soon as this fall."

"This fall?"

"Yes, and now that she's gotten used to the idea that's all she talks about. You'd think she was leaving tomorrow. But Lola's always one to plan ahead."

The front door slammed and Lola came in brushing water from the sleeves of her raincoat. She was flushed with high color and didn't say anything for a few minutes. "Guess who gave me a ride home?"

Seeing the way her eyes sparkled and the rose tint that colored her cheeks, Anna Lee figured it had to be a boy. "Who?" she asked dully.

"Guess."

"We can't imagine who'd be out in this rain," Virginia said. "Tell us."

"Hilton Fields."

"Oh." Virginia's voice seemed to have a catch in it. "Well, that was nice of him. Kept you from getting drenched. I thought he'd left town."

"Mother, you know he lives here now."

"Yes, how could I forget something like that."

"I don't know why you dislike him so."

"I don't dislike him."

"Well, it sure sounds like it. He mentioned you by name, like y'all were friends or something."

"We definitely are not friends."

"He said he gave you a ride home too. Said it looked like it was getting to be a habit to rescue the Edwards women."

"He said that?"

Lola nodded.

"I'd forgotten he gave me a ride, but he's right, he did. Once."

"And he took you to look for ginger ale once," Anna Lee offered.

"You're right. I believe he did. Twice I've been with Mr. Fields."

"Mother! How could anyone forget something like that. Isn't he the most handsome thing you ever saw?"

"I really wasn't paying attention to his looks, Lola. And you shouldn't be either. He's much too old for you to have any interest in."

"How could anybody not have an interest in him? Even you!"

Virginia laughed, and Anna Lee noticed the pink flush on her neck.

"You seem to forget I'm married, my dear. I have a husband and a busybody daughter, so I don't have time to dwell on thoughts of Mr. Hilton Fields."

"Well, I'm NOT married, and he can put his shoes under my bed any night of the week."

"Lola! What a thing to say! And with Anna Lee here."

"I'm only joking. It just means he's handsome, that's all."

"Maybe so, but it sounds awful."

Anna Lee sat up straighter and spoke with quiet authority. "Tyler Rose says he can eat crackers in her bed any old time."

Lola's mouth dropped and they both turned to look at Anna Lee.

"What did you say?"

"Tyler said, . . ."

Virginia laughed. "We know what you said. We're just shocked, that's all."

"The grieving Tyler said that?"

"Don't be nasty, Lola. She's had a hard time of it."

"I know she has, Mother, but you'd think she's made a career of mourning for Stephen. She isn't the only one that's lost somebody in the war."

"No, I suppose in some ways Beatrice feels she lost someone too. Larry just isn't he same since he came back. I wonder that any of them are."

"Mama says the war didn't change Hilton a bit. She says he's no different than he ever was."

"Perhaps not, Anna Lee." Virginia lowered her voice and seemed to speak almost to herself. "Then again, maybe he's different in ways we'll never know."

"Mama says he still has his money, his looks, and his charm. What more could he want?"

Lola's full lips parted slightly. "Someone to love, silly."

"Well, it isn't going to be *you*, silly," Virginia chided, "so just get that out of your head right now. I've told you before, he's old enough to be your father."

"Not by too much." Lola replied dreamily.

"Enough, I assure you."

Anna Lee looked down at her coffee. "Tyler says his hair is white as an angel's wings."

Virginia looked at Anna Lee. "I see nothing angelic about him, not even his hair."

"Maybe because they're in the funeral business and all Tyler just naturally thinks of heavenly things. She still has Stephen's picture on her nightstand even though he's dead."

"Who says he's dead?" Lola spoke from the stove where she poured herself a cup of coffee.

"They think he must be here after all this time. Even Tyler. She says she's quit writing to him."

Lola laughed. "Well, I'd hope so. Writing to a dead man could be awfully uncomfortable if you were sitting on cracker crumbs."

Virginia spoke sternly. "I hope you never experience that kind of grief, Lola, but at least have a little sympathy for those who have."

"I don't want to be mean. She just affects me that way."

"As long as you understand you're being mean."

Anna Lee bent her head low over her cup of coffee the way Lola told her was ill mannered. She didn't care. She lifted the cup with both hands because they were shaking, and she thought for the first time that perhaps Hilton's coming to Bay Harbor wasn't a good thing after all.

Larry Rose had long wondered if his returning to Bay Harbor after the war had been a good thing. He'd brought nothing but heartache with him. Nothing he did pleased Beatrice so he went his own way, trying to reorder his life, searching for ways to cope with his pain. One of the first things he'd done was to look for a place of solitude, a place to escape. That's how he came to build a hideout in the woods behind the old cemetery. It was a way to get away from the house, from the people who came to his office at the funeral home, a place to be alone and calm memories that were etched in fear.

He'd stumbled on the old structure following the trace of a path one day as he tromped through the woods. It was in a small clearing, one room fallen into disrepair. He had no idea how it got there and liked to think it had provided solace to someone from an earlier war. Just the rebuilding had been a balm to his troubled spirit.

He loved the smell of the tall pines, watching them bend in the wind like willowy dancers. The area was pungent with the odor of pine straw and the occasional wood smoke when someone cleared a bit of land. Sunlight tunneled downward between the trees. For Larry it was a benediction.

In order not to arouse suspicion, he went to a nearby town and bought supplies that he took there after dark. He made the structure sound with timber and screen and a new tin roof. What he'd found had been little more than a shell. Now it had a sturdy roof, windows to catch the crosswinds, and a raised floor to discourage snakes.

He furnished it with camping equipment, and after Heather came, added a cot. That it was primitive, little more than a shack, was a great deal of its appeal to Larry. Except in the dead heat of summer or inclement weather, it was comfortable. He even indulged in his youthful passion for art and bought some oil paints. He'd tack a piece of roofing material or cardboard to a tree and lose himself in a picture for long minutes.

As canny as any soldier, he began by taking long walks. He told Beatrice it was good exercise, and eventually no one, not even Anna Lee, thought anything of seeing Larry walking most any place, even toward the dense woods on the outskirts of town.

Heather presented a problem because he couldn't ask her to walk so far. Larry tried to create an air of absentmindedness with Beatrice and began leaving the car parked in back of his office at the funeral home. He'd start out for his routine evening walk and double back to pick up the car.

Heather waited for him in the alley at the back of the boarding house. The first time she'd been frightened, not knowing quite what to expect when she followed him and was swallowed by the midnight woods.

They hadn't gone far when Larry wrapped his handkerchief around a flashlight to guide them. It was the first time they'd been truly alone since she arrived, and the minute he unlocked the door she was in his arms. "Oh God," he moaned, "it's been so long." And then they were lost in a world beyond the scars of war, a world of their own making where he didn't worry about Beatrice and sleepless nights.

Estelle Owens wasn't the only person in Bay Harbor who had trouble sleeping. In a better part of town, Mrs. Richard's expensive Beauty Rest mattress did nothing to assuage Hilton's restless nights.

He couldn't seem to get on with his life and found himself drifting into the same old pattern, having to have a woman, any woman. He knew he had to be more careful if he intended to settle down and have a normal life. Or what he thought was normal.

It was that Edwards woman. She wouldn't leave him alone. It was nothing overt. She just happened to be where he was a little too often. He worried how he'd avoid her once her daughter left for that fancy prep school. She'd have entirely too much time on her hands then. What in God's name made him drive by her house when he couldn't sleep? How did she recognize his car in the dead of night? On his return trip, she was always by the side of the road waiting for him.

"Aren't you afraid your daughter will start asking questions about where you go at night?"

"Lola? No. I've never slept well, and with Darrell having to spend so much time in Washington now that the war's over, she knows I walk on the beach a lot. Sometimes I'm there when the sun comes up."

"Is that so? Hummm. Maybe I could take Lola for a spin without your being any wiser."

"Don't even think about it."

"She'd be a mighty tasty morsel. Young. Innocent . . ."

"Stop it! You don't have any idea what you're talking about. Leave her out of it."

"Oh, I think I have very good idea of what I'm talking about. Is she a talker like her mother? Does she want to tell me what I'm missing beneath her dress, taunt me till I want to tear it off her?"

"If you want to settle down in Bay Harbor, I'd suggest you not even contemplate Lola. I can make your life pure hell."

They were in the back seat, Hilton's head in her lap. He looked up at her in the darkness. "I could do the same for you, Mrs. Edwards, in spades."

"Oh, why are we sitting here fighting like this? We aren't going to hurt anybody. You fill a need for me. I fill one for you."

She didn't fill anything for Hilton, but he wasn't about to tell her that. In one way he felt she was safe. In another, he didn't. She was married so that wasn't an option, and she was older. She was a mother. Still, in some ways she frightened him. How could you trust a woman who'd run out with another man every time her husband left the city limits? There was no telling what she might do.

And yet he kept picking her up and driving to the cemetery where he killed the lights. At first they'd just talked, but it was obvious she wanted more than talk. A lot more. And it wasn't as though they were strangers. She wanted sex, and Hilton wanted someone to hold him. It seemed all backwards but that was the way it was.

People were beginning to talk about him and the Rose girl. She made no effort to hide her interest in him, and they'd gone to the movies a few times. On occasion he'd treat her to a Coke at the drugstore. People probably thought he'd marry her some day. But she was so young. In not too many years he'd be pushing forty. Too young, she was much too young. She was beautiful in a feline kind of way, but she wasn't for him any more than the Edwards woman was. But he wasn't about to let her know that, not any more than he'd let Virginia know it. He'd learned a long time ago not to burn his bridges.

Hilton sensed Virginia's jealousy of Tyler, and he had no scruples about using it against her. A married woman with a daughter, he knew she wouldn't dare be overt. Taunting her could be the highlight of his day.

Hilton was never more affectionate with Tyler than when Virginia was present. If Virginia and Tyler happened to be in the same store, Hilton would give a cursory wave to Virginia and rush up to Tyler, taking her hand in both of his, often planting a kiss on her cheek. He knew what this did to Virginia, but he never dreamed of the effect it had on love-struck Tyler.

One night when he was with Virginia he saw a light in the woods. He backed the car out and took her home right then even though she insisted he was imagining things. She hadn't seen a light and accused him of wanting to get rid of her. He wanted to get rid of her all right, but he had seen a light of some kind.

After he dropped Virginia off at one of the cuts to the beach—she always walked home from the beach, barefoot and windblown, in case Lola were to wake up when she came in—he was too keyed up to go home. He pulled in at the park and walked out on the pier. Feeling his way past the missing planks, his footsteps sounded loud in the darkness, loud and alone. The water looked black and forbidding. It suited his mood. He hated himself for being unable to find the peace he sought, the happiness and security that come, not from money, but from belonging to someone you love.

In the furthest reaches of his soul, he felt he'd been cursed by women. Maybe the ideal woman, the one who'd spark his heart, didn't exist. Robert and Estelle seemed happy enough, and Hilton knew better than anyone that Estelle hadn't been Robert's first choice. Robert had served time in the sufferance of his love for Grace.

Hilton ground his teeth, feeling less than a man for this search, for this longing for his romantic ideal. He was a man, a veteran, not some silly schoolgirl. Maybe he should take a closer look at the Rose girl, really get to know her.

CHAPTER
Fifteen

August 1946

Hilton was just pulling in the drive of his mother's house when Robert drove up behind him. Hilton rushed over and got in the car with Robert. "Come on. I want to show you something."

Hilton had Robert drive a few miles out of town. "This is it, Robert. I bought this land. I can walk on my own piece of Bay Harbor now."

Robert whistled. "I never noticed this before, Hil. Thought Bay Harbor had only two hills. Course I wasn't looking for a place to build, but damn, it's pretty. Reminds me of the woods where we grew up."

"Me too. That's why I had to have it. I like to imagine my own son exploring these woods some day."

"You're still crazy about children?"

"More than ever. I'll build a big house and fill it with children."

Stakes had been driven in the ground marking the three acre parcel across from the Bay. Stooping to avoid branches, watching for snakes, they walked the perimeter. It was heavily wooded with ancient oaks, pines, giant magnolia, cottonwood, palms, wild holly, and juniper. There was a bit of a breeze, enough to perfume the air with magnolia blossoms and the baked odor of sun warmed pine needles.

"I feel almost guilty at the thought of cutting any of this. I'll take out only enough for a house."

"Thick as it is, there'll be plenty left. I just cain't get over how pretty it is.

What's your mother think of it?"

"She hasn't seen it yet. I wanted you to be the first."

"Well, you've got the best looking property in Bay Harbor, Hil."

"That's what I think. Now I have to find the prettiest girl to live on it with me."

"That shouldn't be a problem for you, but I know it is. You've waited so long. Everything has to be perfect."

Hilton nodded. "Yeah, I guess that's what I want all right. But finding this property was a lot easier job, believe me."

"Maybe so, but the chase is always fun. Always." Robert squatted, resting on his heels, snapped a piece of grass and put it in his mouth. He looked away from Hilton, up toward the treetops. "I got me a problem, Hil."

"That right?"

"Yep. It's a woman at one of the boarding houses I stay at, a young widow."

Hilton let out a low whistle. "I hadn't figured on something like this."

"Me neither. Hil, she reminds me of Grace."

"God, Robert, I'm sorry. That has to hurt. Anything happened between you?"

"Naw. Not yet. Almost though. I knocked on her door one night long after bedtime. She answered wearing a loose robe, her hair hanging almost to her waist. She didn't say anything. Neither did I. She knew what I wanted. I just turned and walked away."

"Robert, this isn't the same as when we were young. You got more at stake now. You know that."

"That's why I walked away."

"Does she know you're married?"

"Yes."

"If she'd let you in, would you have thought less of her?"

"I don't know. I'd sure love to have found out though."

"Maybe you better stay some place else from now on. At least until you get it all worked out in your mind. Have you considered that you aren't being fair to the widow lady, that she isn't Grace? I know this is a hurt that won't leave you, but you must understand that this isn't something you can just act on and then leave."

"I know that. You're right. Looks like God never meant me to have Grace. She marries my own brother, my twin. And now they're both dead. I was never meant to have her."

"God gave you Anna Lee, Robert."

"He did that. I hope to God Anna Lee never finds out she was a mistake. If Grace hadn't been so sick, if she hadn't thought I was Earl, Anna Lee would never have existed."

"You had that one night . . ."

"Yes, that one moment, and it wasn't even me. I was my twin brother for one quick moment."

"Have you ever considered what it meant to Grace though? She thought she had her husband again. She had her moment too."

"Did you ever tell Estelle?"

"You think I got a death wish? Hell no. She'd never have accepted Anna Lee. She thinks it was Johnn."

"Johnn!"

"Yeah, Johnn was always hanging around Grace like a sick puppy. Estelle thinks Johnn is Anna Lee's real daddy. I admit I encouraged her to think that. I told her Johnn was single, not daddy material, and she agreed we'd adopt the baby, give her a home."

"Good god, Robert, what a mess. Sir Walter Scott said it best—*Oh what a tangled web we weave, when first we practice to deceive.*"

"Jesus, Hil. You quoting poetry to me?"

"My paper route wasn't my only means of making money. My mother used to pay me to memorize poems. You know, schoolteacher stuff. Scott was a favorite of hers. Don't let on I told you that, and I wouldn't want her to know I came to like some of them myself. Anyway, women like it. A few lines of verse in a woman's ear and you'll be in her pants like greased lightning. But don't you go trying it on the widow lady."

Robert blew his nose and looked up at the sky. "I'll stay someplace else."

In the end Hilton couldn't let his dream go to a builder and decided to be his own contractor. As soon as the lot was cleared of enough trees to make room for a house, he went to the Florida Power Company to get an electrical hook up. He walked in the door and knew he was on the brink of something that could change his life.

At first he thought no one was around, but when he approached the counter he saw a rather tall woman bent from the waist looking through the bottom drawer of an oak filing cabinet. He didn't say a word as he looked at the curve of her hip and the shapely legs exposed below the hem of her navy blue skirt. He was savoring the view when Horace Beard came out of his office and saw Hilton standing at the counter.

"Anything I can do for you, Hilton?"

Heather let out a discreet "Oh" and stood up. "Truly I'm so sorry. I didn't hear you come in, sir."

"Obviously." Hilton smiled and noted the flush that heightened her charms.

Horace was a man not given to a woman's charms or a man's stature in the community. A confirmed bachelor, he'd lived with his mother until she died, and now he worked by the book and went home at noon each day to shave and avoid five o'clock shadow. He cleared his throat and, with a gesture familiar to almost everyone in Bay Harbor, touched his face to measure the growth of his beard. "Is there something I can do for you?" he repeated.

"There absolutely is," Hilton answered without taking his eyes from Heather. "Please introduce me to this lovely young lady."

"That's Heather . . . Mrs. Rushby."

"Hilton Fields," he replied without waiting to be introduced.

"Pleased," she said and gave a brief nod.

"Was that Miss or Mrs. Rushby?"

"Mrs.," she answered.

Hilton couldn't hide his downcast expression, and Heather's eyes widened slightly, she smiled, and resumed her filing.

There was an awkward silence, and Horace tried again. "Do you have business with us, Hilton?"

"Oh, yes. I surely do." He looked at Heather and smiled. "Very important business."

Forty-five minutes later he'd completed the necessary forms and could delay his departure no longer. He started out the door but turned for one last look at Heather. She covered her mouth to stifle laughter when he bumped into a girl on the sidewalk.

Hilton grabbed the girl by the shoulders to steady her. "I'm sorry. Oh, my lord, Anna Lee. I didn't hurt you, did I?"

"No, sir. You just startled me."

"Anna Lee, do you know Mrs. Rushby?" He inclined his head back toward Horace Beard's office.

"Heather? Sure. She used to work at the drugstore."

"I don't recall seeing her."

"She was part time and didn't work there very long."

Hilton kept stroking his chin with his left hand. He seemed about to ask a question when T. J. raced between them on his bike, just missing Hilton's foot. He hit the brakes a few feet away and waited.

"Friend of yours?" Hilton asked.

"Yes, sir."

"He needs to learn some manners. Hey, buddy, you better ride that bike on the street before you hurt somebody. That wasn't cute."

"Yes, sir, I will, sir." He stopped short of saluting.

Hilton ignored the sarcastic tone, and decided to let it go. He offered Anna Lee a ride home, but T. J. was waiting for her. As soon as Hilton drove off she walked up to him. "That wasn't nice."

"I thought I had more room."

"Those tires seem to hold air okay now."

"Yeah, but they're so skinny I can't ride on the beach." He began boosting himself up to the seat, one foot on a pedal. "Death tour tonight at nine o'clock. Dad was just called out of town. Think you can get out of the house?"

"I can make it."

"Okay, see you then."

Anna Lee watched him ride off. Here she'd turned down a ride from Hilton and T. J. didn't offer her one. There was only a tiny fender over the back tire, but she could sit on the crossbar.

She'd walked less than a block when Hilton came by and tapped the horn lightly. She started toward the car, and he pulled to the curb, leaned over and opened the door for her. She looked around to see if anyone was watching. There wasn't a girl in Bay Harbor who wouldn't like to be alone in the car with Hilton Fields.

"Hilton, would you mind saying something to Mama sometime about me using your first name?"

"She doesn't believe I told you to?"

"No, sir. I have to call you Mr. Fields at home."

"Leave it to me. I'll say something next time I'm in the drugstore." He cleared his throat. "Do you know where the Rushbys live?"

"Yes, sir."

"Would you mind telling me where that would be?"

"Oh yes, sir. At the boarding house."

"The boarding house!"

"You know, Helen's, across from the drugstore."

"I know where it is. I'm just surprised, that's all. Do you know Mr. Rushby?"

"No, sir." She stared at the steering wheel. A slight tremor was still evident in his left hand.

By the time they pulled up in front of her house, she'd slipped her shoes off and had her feet on the dashboard.

"Why do you like to sit like that?"

"I don't know. I just like to, and Lola says when I'm thirteen I can't do things like that any more. This may be the last time I get to do it."

"I almost forgot Robert said you had a birthday next week. What's your birthstone?"

"Peridot."

"Peridot, huh?"

"Yes, sir. Green's my favorite color. Except that Mama might let me wear natural lipstick, I kinda dread being thirteen though. I won't be able to get in the picture show for a dime any more, and I'll have to be more ladylike."

Hilton smiled. "We all have our crosses to bear, but I thought the price went up when you were twelve."

"It does, but I've been saying for the past year that I'm big for my age."

"I may not be a good judge of age, but I'm a good judge of women. Sit still a minute and close your eyes." He reached into the glove compartment and took out a small box.

"Keep your eyes closed and hold out your hand." He placed the velvet box on her outstretched palm. "Okay. You can look now."

She opened the lid and gasped when she saw the gold locket set with a brilliant peridot. "You didn't forget. You even knew my birthstone."

"I didn't forget, but I intended to wait until your birthday. We'll keep it a secret until the big day. Okay?"

"Yes, sir!" Anna Lee threw her arms around his neck. "It's the best present ever."

"Worth paying a quarter to get in the picture show?"

"Oh yes, sir. More than that even."

Hilton was laughing when Anna Lee got out of the car and watched him backing away. He hit the brake when she walked up to his window. "Do you want me to tell you why I don't know Mr. Rushby?"

"As a matter of fact, I'd love to know the answer to that question, smarty."

"There isn't a Mr. Rushby."

"There isn't . . ."

"No, sir. He was killed in the war."

Hilton leaned over and gave Anna Lee a big kiss. She stood with her hand on her cheek long after he drove away.

CHAPTER
Sixteen

Friday Evening

Estelle sat on the living room sofa crocheting another white tablecloth and listening to a program on the Philco radio that occupied a full corner of the room. She had pins stuck in her pattern book to mark her place, and her fingers were a blur of movement. Anna Lee figured she was mad because Robert had gone to see Hilton. From the safe distance of the kitchen, Anna Lee called that she was going to see T. J. and would be right back.

Her mother didn't even look up. She stabbed the crochet needle repeatedly into the threads of the tablecloth. Estelle had found the bracelet wrapped in Robert's underwear.

The darkness didn't faze Anna Lee. It was black as a mortician's apron, and the sparkle of stars piercing the void traveled too many light years to brighten a moonless night. She tiptoed up the steps of the funeral home and joined the other children sitting with their backs against the porch railing, facing the door, waiting for a signal from T. J.

Bodies shifted position, shoes pushed against the floorboards, but nobody said a word. They knew Mary Rose was in the apartment upstairs, and they'd rather be found by T. J.'s dad than Mary. She gave them their shots after all.

The beam of T. J.'s flashlight grew brighter as he came up the hall and neared the door, but nobody moved until he whistled. One by one he beamed the light in their faces.

"Everybody here knows the rules, don't they?"

Nobody answered. They hardly dared breathe as they filed into the room, made darker by the blackout shades T. J. had lowered. A breeze from the giant fans pushed the shades tight against the windows.

Somebody whispered. "Did any more bodies explode?"

"Not this week they ain't." T. J. slid the dimes from the table and turned to face his audience. A born showman, his chest swelled with the importance of the information he was able to share.

"If anybody here is ever in a hospital, you'll know what to expect. They'll lay you out on a table." He slid the fingers of his left hand down the metal surface. "It'll be padded, of course, and they'll have an instrument table on wheels like this one." There was the sound of metal on metal as he pushed the instruments to one side.

"Any of y'all want to be an undertaker when they grow up?" The room was silent except for the hum of the fans. "Well, if you do, it's a good job. If by some miracle people ever quit dying, you could always work in a beauty parlor or maybe be a barber. Hair don't know you're dead. It just keeps on growing. My dad cuts hair and lots of time has to shave the men. He got cosmetology training at the morticians' college in Nashville."

One of the boys said, "My aunt owns a beauty parlor in Tallahassee."

"Can she embalm bodies?"

"No."

"Well, my dad can do both. He just got a new kit, and I found his old one in the garbage." He reached down for a case that he placed on the instrument table. He snapped the lid open to reveal a tray of cosmetics. "Come over here and look at the colors." He lifted the lids off the containers. "See, there's colors for all skin tones, a pinkish red for rouge, and a real pretty pale blue. You know how people are always saying a dead person looks so natural? Well, this is why. It's makeup. There's even powder in here."

One of the girls asked, "Does it smell good?"

T. J. laughed. "It don't smell. You don't go around smelling dead people, dummy."

They formed a line and filed past the table. One of the boys started to stick his finger in the case when T. J. grabbed his hand. "You wantin' me to make you up, Freddie?" Silence. "You know better than to touch anything. Who thinks I should make him up?" Freddie walked away and began rattling the doorknob.

"It's locked. Who wants to hold Freddie?"

There was nervous laughter and a shuffling of feet.

Anna Lee knew T. J. was mad and wondered if boys had puberty too. She was afraid things might get rough and if anything was broken that'd be the end of the death tours. She heard herself saying, "No, do me. Make me up, T. J."

"Aw, Anna Lee . . ."

"I mean it. I'd really like it. It'll be fun. Make me look like a movie star."

In a soft whisper, a young girl suggested, "Elizabeth Taylor!"

One of the boys called out, "No, Mickey Rooney."

"That's enough. Shut up." T. J. turned on more lights.

Anna Lee sat on a stool and T. J. went to work. He dipped his fingers in the cream and began applying makeup to her face. He chose a pinkish beige color to look more natural. He dabbed blue under her eyes. When he'd covered her face, he drew arching eyebrows and applied rouge.

There was quiet laughter. Someone said, "She looks like a booby star."

"Well, maybe I applied too much." T. J. began rubbing her face with a piece of gauze. It became a palette of color, the rouge mixing with the skin tones and turning orange. He got some of the eyebrow pencil off, but her skin held tight to the tint of death. He kept wiping his palms on his pants, and Anna Lee grew tense listening to his labored breathing.

Somebody snickered. "Give her a mirror."

"I ain't got a mirror. Wait a minute, Anna Lee."

T. J.'s hands were shaking so much he had trouble unlocking the door. He dropped the key twice before he was able to open get it unlocked. "And the first one that opens his damn mouth about this won't never come back, you hear me! Now go home."

He didn't have to tell them twice. This was probably the most frightening thing that had ever happened, and they took off running. The last girl out of the door looked back and said, "I like it when you curse, T. J."

Anna Lee hadn't worried all that much until T. J. turned and started back toward her. His freckles glistened with tears. "God, Anna Lee, I don't know what to do. My dad's gonna kill me. He'll be back early tomorrow morning, and I'll ask him for something that'll remove it." T. J. took all the money out of his pocket and handed it to her. "I didn't know it wouldn't come off, honest."

Anna Lee was too frightened to answer. She sat on the stool with her shoulders hunched forward and her knees pressed together. *How bad do I look, really? Will it wear off before I'm 13? Will Mama beat me?* And then she grew calm and unafraid. *They put this on my mother. It's okay because they put it on my mother. She could see the coffin, her mother laying there, her eyes closed as though she was sleeping. She wore a dress the color of the blue makeup, and she was beautiful. Like a movie star. I'm closer to her now. I know I am.*

"You okay, Anna Lee? Why are you smiling?"

"It'll be all right, T. J. I told you to. You don't have to tell your dad even." She put the handful of dimes on the table, hooked her pinky finger around T. J.'s for a moment, and walked into night.

Anna Lee tiptoed into the house and went to the bathroom. She'd hardly closed the door when Estelle called, "Is that you, Anna Lee?"

"Yes 'em."

"What are you doing?"

"I don't feel good. I'm going to the bathroom."

"School starts in a few weeks. I'll get some castor oil and clean you out good."

Just the thought made Anna Lee truly ill. She'd been standing with her back to the door, eyes closed, but now she walked over to the toilet and flushed it.

"I don't need any castor oil, Mama. I'm fine. Really."

"We'll see."

The bathroom was stifling. One small window sat high on the outside wall so people couldn't see in. There was an old claw-foot bathtub, a toilet, a mirrored medicine cabinet over the sink, and shelves for towels. The room was cramped and the air stale.

When she couldn't put it off any longer, she turned to look in the mirror over the washbasin. No wonder T. J. cried. She began crying too, tears that slid down her face like oil on glass. *My mother didn't look like this. I bet she looked like Greer Garson.* The blue makeup under her eyes had a purplish cast, and the rest of her face was pinkish orange. The remains of the eyebrow pencil were more like lightning strikes than eyebrows. She flushed the toilet again.

I have the face of a movie star all right. The bride of Frankenstein—after she died. Why did I insist he do me? T. J. would have still liked me even if I hadn't volunteered. And I'd give up death tours to keep from looking this way. Mama'll kill me.

She spread a thick layer of Pond's cold cream over her face and stared at her wide eyes and pale lips the mirror. Now I look like Al Jolson! She put her face close to the mirror and smiled. She spread her arms wide and sang, "Mammy, how I love you, how I . . ."

"Anna Lee, did you call me?"

"No ma'am." She flushed the toilet again and then dampened a wash cloth with water and began rubbing. She found her own eyebrows beneath the dark pencil lines T. J. had drawn, but the color on her face was a pale pumpkin, and the purplish cast under her eyes lightened some but still looked sickly.

What if it never comes off? What am I going to tell Mama? She'll never let me wear natural lipstick now. Anna Lee put on her gown and crawled into bed. Despite the heat, she pulled the sheet over her head and prayed for sleep.

"Night, Mama."

"Night, baby," Estelle called. From the muffled sound of her voice, Anna Lee could tell she was holding straight pins in her mouth.

She knew Larry worked most Saturdays and fell asleep hoping he could help her. She didn't sleep much, and Saturday morning she was up early enough to make coffee and fill her thermos before Estelle and Robert were out of bed. She dressed and put on Lola's raincoat, pulling the hood over her head. She'd almost made it out the door when Estelle saw her.

"Where do you think you're going?"

Anna Lee didn't turn around. "I don't know. Maybe to see T. J. or Tyler."

"Don't be long. We've got work to do this morning. Your daddy threw me a curve ball last night. Two of 'em in fact. And why in God's name do you have on that raincoat?"

"I thought I heard thunder."

"I didn't hear thunder, and you're going to burn up in that thing. It's hot out already."

Without turning around, she took the raincoat off and draped it over her arm, concealing the thermos. Still with her back to Estelle, she started down the steps.

"Did you have breakfast?"

"Yes, ma'am. I won't be long." She started running then before Estelle could call her back.

She was sitting on the stoop when Larry got to his office. "Anna Lee?" He leaned over and peered at her face. "What in the world happened to you?"

"Can you help me, please? I found Mr. Foster's cosmetology kit in the garbage and thought it was makeup."

"Let's have some of that coffee you have there and see if we can come up with a plan."

They listened for Foster and when they heard his car drive up, Larry went out and talked to him. He came back with a small jar of liquid. "This may burn but it'll take some of the orange away. Foster says it'll wear off, but it's real old and that's why it's staining your face."

It burned all right, but Anna Lee never said a word. She sat in the chair she'd come to think of as Heather's. She shut her eyes tight and Larry dipped cotton into the liquid and rubbed her face vigorously.

When he finished she was a pale shade of pumpkin. Her face hurt so much she could hardly open her mouth to talk.

"Seeing how your mama is such an expert with a switch we better come up with a good story for this, something to explain the orange glow."

"I hate it when my friends tell me they can hear me screaming when she whips me. Can you hear me?"

"I'm sorry to say I can, honey. But we'll think of something. Don't worry."

They sipped their coffee and offered up suggestions they discarded almost as soon as they thought of them.

"Hilton told me a proverb. It says that all truth is good but not all truth is good to say."

"I wasn't aware Mr. Fields was into proverbs."

"Oh, yes. He's always reading poetry and things to improve his mind."

"Is that so? Well, he's got a ways to go. Sorry, Anna Lee, I know he's your dad's friend. I've just never liked the guy. I will admit his proverb fits this situation."

"Daddy says Hilton has a good heart. He's always trying to help people in need."

"That right?"

"Yes, sir. He gives lots of money to the Red Cross, and if any of the people who work for him get sick or run into trouble, he makes sure they get taken care of. He doesn't talk about it though. He doesn't like people to know."

Larry was in no mood to give Hilton any ground no matter how much he did for charity. He ignored what she'd told him and gave Anna Lee a hard look. He took her chin between his thumb and forefinger and turned her face from side to side.

Anna Lee held her breath. Finally he snapped his fingers. "I got it! We'll tell Estelle you've been eating a lot of carrots to make your eyes stronger. What you have here, young lady, is jaundice from eating too many carrots. If she doesn't believe you, I'll talk to her."

Anna Lee smiled and settled back to enjoy her coffee.

Beatrice Rose made a fresh pot of coffee after Larry went to the funeral home, but now she sat at the kitchen table letting it grow cold. Larry wouldn't even have coffee with her on Saturday morning. More and more she felt like a widow. She wore an old yellow wrapper over her gown and her bare feet rested on the cool linoleum. She listened to the faucet dripping in the kitchen sink, the measured tick of a time bomb.

At last she understood why her parents drank. She didn't know what they'd wanted to escape, but she knew hard liquor could be a temporary cure. She held the coffee cup with both hands and trembled as she fought to keep from throwing it across the room.

Her life with Larry was over. She had to accept that. The only time he talked to her anymore was to complain about something. He found fault with everything. She couldn't even cook an egg to suit him. She'd reasoned with him, had tried unsuccessfully to force an interest in his life scenes. She even thought to enliven their social life and surprise him by inviting the English woman to dinner. What a disaster that had been. Larry wouldn't even look at Heather. He couldn't have been more unfriendly or disinterested.

Heather was gracious and sweet, but Beatrice had wanted to fall through the floor with embarrassment. Larry stared at his plate and refused to join the conversation Tyler struggled to keep going.

Beatrice eased her grip on her coffee cup and raised it to her lips. It was as lacking in warmth as her husband. She threw the cup against the stove and left the room. Coffee dripped to the floor, pooling around the shards of glass. She had an uneasy feeling that had nothing to do with the mess she left in the kitchen.

Beatrice dressed, moving her belt to the last notch. Diets had never worked for her, but the stress she'd been under since Larry got home took the weight off quicker than an illness. She walked to town because Larry had the car at the funeral home again, and she wasn't about to go after it.

Beatrice was a stranger to the two barrooms in town, O'Kelly's and Brady's. Never having been in either one, she chose Brady's since it was closer. She hesitated in the door and squinted against the dark. There was a mirror behind the oak bar and below were rows of bottles with names like Jim Beam and Seagram's 7. She could see tea colored liquid in some but it was so dark she couldn't read the contents. Bats, she thought, the men who come in here have to be a bunch of bats. She drew a deep breath, inhaling the familiar salty odor of beer and smoke that passersby smelled every time they walked down the sidewalk past the bar.

It was ten o'clock on a Saturday morning, and already she could hear the soft click of balls from the poolroom in the back. There were two other people at the bar. By afternoon the place would be hopping.

One of the men at the bar yelled, "Hey Brady, you got a customer."

"Yes, ma'am?"

Beatrice fumbled in her purse and remembered her mother had favored gin so she ordered a bottle of Tanqueray.

"An entire bottle?"

"Yes, please."

"You want a glass?"

Beatrice laughed. "Oh, no. No. I'll take it with me." With the confidence of a regular customer, she looked Brady in the eye, or where she thought his eyes should be, and counted out her money. She tucked the brown paper bag under her arm and walked back into the welcome light of a sunny day.

Virginia Edwards came out of the drugstore as Beatrice approached. She stared at the bag, but Beatrice made no attempt to conceal it.

"You're out mighty early, Beatrice."

"I could say the same for you."

"We're sending Lola to a college prep school in the fall, and I'm buying toiletries and the like."

"We've given up hope of getting Tyler to go to college. Glad you're having more luck with Lola. Good seeing you." Beatrice lifted her chin, sucked in her stomach and continued home, purse swinging, the sack secured under her arm.

She was nearly home when Estelle Owens waved to her from Robert's old black Ford. She'd never realized Saturday mornings were so busy, that so many women were either going to town or coming home.

Beatrice's determination hadn't faltered as she dropped her purse on a table in the hall and went straight to the kitchen. She searched the cabinet for a small glass. She chose one that had held Kraft's cream cheese spread. Glass crunched underfoot as she walked across the broken coffee cup. She sat at the kitchen table and stared at the brown coffee stains on the stove and linoleum. The gin tasted worse than cold coffee.

When Tyler found her, she was clutching an empty glass, wondering if maybe she should have eaten something first.

"Mother! What happened? Are you okay?"

Beatrice let her head drop to the table and began to snore.

Tyler started a fresh pot of coffee, put the Tanqueray in the cabinet, and cleaned up the spilled coffee and broken glass, careful not to soil her new red slacks. She considered letting Beatrice sleep it off but was afraid she might fall off the chair. She made oven toast before she roused her, convincing her to drink some coffee and eat the thick slices of buttered bread. They sat in silence while Beatrice drank two cups of coffee and finished off the toast.

Beatrice dabbed her mouth with a napkin and turned to Tyler as though they'd been having a casual conversation. Her tongue was only a little thick. "Tyler, don't ever marry a man who has never had a girlfriend other than you."

Tyler shook her head as though to clear her thoughts. "Ma'am?"

"You heard me. Never be your husband's only girlfriend."

"Don't tell me you were the only girl Dad ever dated."

"That's right."

"I don't believe you. Really? You never said so before."

"Never thought it mattered before."

"And it matters now?"

"Oh, yes, now I think it does. And he was so young, younger than me, you know. I knew what people were saying, but I didn't care. I wanted him more than I'd ever wanted anything in my life. Your father was unbearably shy and had no idea how handsome he'd become."

"You were pretty too, Mother."

"I didn't have the good looks your father did. I looked okay. Youth has its own beauty. Youth on a plain girl is something to behold. I should have been wary, I guess, knowing he'd never dated, much less kissed a girl."

"Dad had never kissed a girl?"

"Never. We were sitting in his car in front of my house one night. We'd been going together quite some time by then. It was dark out, no moon, or I'd never have had the courage. I just came right out with it. "Larry," I said, "when are you going to kiss me?"

"I couldn't believe I'd asked him that, but he answered me right away. 'Bea, I've never kissed a girl' he said, and forward girl that I was, I moved over next to him and said, I'll show you how to kiss a girl. And boy did I show him. Knowing that I was the first, I should have realized I was taking a chance, but I fell in love with him and nothing else mattered."

"But I still don't understand . . ."

"Well, if a man's been with only one woman, he's always going to wonder what else is out there. Would someone else have been better. Is someone better . . ."

"But what about the woman? What if he's her only fella?"

"It's different with a woman. Women don't need to shop and compare."

"Oh, Mother, don't be silly." Tyler got up and refilled their cups.

"A wife will always wonder if her husband is regretting his lack of experience, but a woman doesn't need that."

"Who says?"

"I say. A man will always wonder, but one man is enough for a woman."

Tyler sipped her coffee. "Now, mother, do you really believe men and women are so different?"

"I know so. And you should too. You're not a child any more. But for that awful war, you'd be married now. And, Tyler, beware of a fault finding man. It's usually his weakness coming out to hurt you." She looked around, realizing the Tanqueray and her glass were missing.

"Darling, do me a favor. Get that bottle of gin and pour it down the drain. No matter how miserable I am, I'm not going to take that path. I've seen where it leads. I had a weak moment, that's all."

CHAPTER
Seventeen

On Friday night while Estelle crocheted and Anna Lee was having her complexion altered, Hilton was trying to convince Robert that the Owens should ask him and the widow Rushby over for supper the following night.

Robert frowned. "That's mighty short notice, Hil."

"She's a widow living at a boarding house. What else has she got to do?"

"No, I meant for Estelle. She's gone be on the warpath over this."

"Tell her I begged you to do it, that I was nearly in tears. A woman can't stand to think of a man crying. And I'll get my mom's Annie to come help her serve the meal."

"I'll see what I can do. Estelle'd like having a maid all right. I'll tell her to invite Heather first thing tomorrow morning."

When Anna Lee came home from Larry's that morning Estelle seemed to be everywhere at once. "Put those groceries away, Anna Lee, and then get the beds made. We're having company tonight, and we have to get this place in shape. I want this house clean by noon so I can start cooking."

Anna Lee didn't even ask who but busied herself and was able to avoid being in the same room with her mother for a good hour. Estelle was cleaning the toilet when Anna Lee walked into the bathroom. Before she could walk away, Estelle saw her.

"Aaaiieee!"

Anna Lee froze, afraid to move.

"What in God's name is wrong with your face? What've you done to yourself?"

"It's . . . it's jaundice, Mama."

"Jaundice, my ass." She grabbed Anna Lee by the shoulders and peered at her face. "Get that stuff off right this minute."

"I can't. It won't come off, Mama."

"Get it off or I'll beat you within an inch of your life."

Anna Lee began crying. "Ask Mr. Larry. He said he'd tell you. I kept carrots at his office. Ask him."

Estelle stomped out the back door and went straight to Larry's office. She didn't bother to knock.

Larry took one look at her and started explaining. "Estelle, you know how kids are. Anna Lee saw an article in a magazine at the drugstore about how good carrots are for your eyes. She said you were always fussing at her for reading in poor light so she was going to improve her eyesight with carrots. I guess she ate too many."

Estelle's mouth was shut tight and she was breathing hard. "She hasn't done anything that dumb since she was three years old and stuffed a pea up her nose."

Larry started laughing, and after a few minutes Estelle did too. "I guess if she never does anything worse . . ." She looked around his office at all the sketches. "I've heard people talking about how nice these are. You're providing a real service, Larry, getting people to thinking about living instead of dying, helping them find some meaning in their lives."

"Thanks, Estelle. I'm just sorry I didn't pay more attention to Anna Lee and those carrots."

"Well, don't let her be a nuisance."

"She's good company."

"How long do you think this jaundice will last?"

"Not more than a week I wouldn't think—if she doesn't eat any more carrots. It's nothing to worry about. Really. Your time could be better spent thinking about your window displays. I haven't noticed you doing anything provocative lately. I always enjoyed your insights into the community."

"Well, those insights can get you into a peck of trouble sometimes, but I'm flattered that you noticed my work, you being a real artist and all."

"I wish we could talk longer, Estelle, but I really must get back to work. And I'm sorry about the jaundice. I should have been more observant."

Estelle started for the door and stopped. "How's Tyler getting along, Larry?"

"Fine. It's been rough, but I think she's going to be just fine."

"I'm glad. You know, people are beginning to talk about her and Hilton. Maybe he's helping her get over Stephen. They'd make a handsome couple all right."

She left, and Larry dropped into his chair and sat speechless, staring at the door.

Shielded by a tall hedge of ligustrum, Anna Lee had been squatting underneath Larry's window listening to see if Estelle bought the jaundice story. She waited until she was sure her mother was out of sight before she stood up and looked through the dusty screen. Larry's back was to her. She was about to say something to him when the door opened, and Anna Lee ducked. She heard Heather call Larry darling. She was sure she said darling. Bent from the waist like T. J., Anna Lee began running away from something she couldn't escape.

Heather paced up and down her small room at the boarding house. There was just enough space for a single bed and dresser so even pacing was confined. Every day it seemed more like a cell. Was it going to take a scandal to make Larry divorce Beatrice?

People were trying to entwine her in their lives, and she didn't like it. The last thing she wanted was to have dinner with the Owens.

She was caught totally unaware when Estelle came by that morning and begged her to come to dinner the very same evening. It was rude to give an invitation on short notice like that, but Heather couldn't very well plead an active social life. Things had been a bit testy between her and Estelle so she rather enjoyed watching her beg. In the end Heather promised she'd be there by six o'clock, silently praying the sneaky Anna Lee wouldn't be there as well. Once she and Larry were married, Anna Lee would no longer be welcome at his office. She'd see to that.

Heather had to get word to Larry that she couldn't meet him that night as usual so later that morning she followed the back roads to his office. They embraced briefly, but she didn't even sit down. When he asked why she had to change their plans, Foster came in before she could reply. *How many times could she pretend to be there on business?*

About three o'clock that afternoon Helen came to Heather's room to give her a phone message. Hilton Fields would be by at five forty-five to give her a ride to the Owens.

"Hilton Fields?"

"Yes, his mother lives here, but Hilton's moved here only since the war. You may have seen him, a tall, slender . . ."

"Yes, I think I know who you mean. He was in the office just yesterday. I didn't realize he was invited to the Owens as well."

"Maybe it was a last minute thing, but Hilton and Robert Owens are like that." Helen held up two fingers pressed tightly together.

Heather smiled and shrugged. "Oh, well."

She waited in one of the rockers on the upstairs screened porch of the boarding house. When she saw Hilton get out of his car, she started toward the stairs, and they arrived at the landing at the same time.

"This is very kind, you know. Mr. Fields, is it?"

"Just Hilton, and it's my pleasure to be of help." He stepped aside and let her walk down the stairs ahead of him. In the car he was silent, and made no attempt at small talk. When they passed Tyler's house she waved, and he and Heather both waved back. Hilton laughed, "I guess we have a mutual friend."

Heather smiled. "Her family has been very kind to me."

"I'm sure they have. The Roses are mighty fine people, just like the Owens. Robert and Estelle want you to feel welcome too."

Estelle put out her best dishes, the ones she'd accumulated from the coupons she earned buying Standard coffee. The Rogers Brothers silver plate was scratched but that couldn't be helped, and she had nice goblets Johnn and Amy had given them for Christmas. She'd never served a meal on her crocheted tablecloth but decided the occasion called for it. She smoothed its intricate field of white flowers over the mahogany table with loving strokes. Every stitch came from her own fingers. She hoped Hilton and Heather knew enough to be impressed.

The house smelled of furniture polish, fresh flowers were on the table, and she bought green tapers for the candle holders Johnn bought her back in the days when they made bets on the war. She felt good about the way things looked, and it was a good thing. Nothing else went right.

Robert opened the screen door and waited as Heather and Hilton came up the front steps. Anna Lee stood to one side and watched Heather raise her eyebrows when she saw her. Anna Lee gave her most innocent smile, looked her in the eye and said, "Mr. Larry says it's jaundice. It isn't catching."

"That's good to know."

"Yes. Mr. Larry doesn't have it." Did she imagine the look of unfriendliness in Heather's eyes?

Hilton knelt down and took a closer look at her. "Your timing's off, darlin'. You'd be the hit of Halloween."

Estelle put a pitcher of iced tea on the sideboard. "That's the truth, Hilton. Let's just hope it's gone before school starts."

"Well, even if it isn't, Anna Lee can handle it. I hope I have a daughter with her spunk some day."

As Hilton had promised, his mother's maid, Annie, served the food, and was to clean up afterwards. Even with help, or perhaps because of it, Estelle was agitated and jumpy.

Hilton was his usual gallant self and complimented Estelle profusely on the good food she'd prepared. The rest of the time everybody seemed to tiptoe around asking Heather questions.

Heather was generally quiet and noncommittal. Anna Lee had been warned to keep her mouth shut, which was really too bad since she was filled with questions she swallowed down with the pork roast and potato salad heaped in Estelle's cut-glass bowl. She looked over at Hilton seated beside Heather, and he winked at her.

After dinner Annie served coffee and Estelle's memorable coconut pie. The only sound was the scrape of forks on china when Estelle broke the silence. "Heather, we're so sorry about your loss. If we can do anything to help . . ."

"My loss? Oh, you mean my husband. Yes, it remains painful even yet."

"We're sorry about your dead baby too."

They all turned and looked at Anna Lee. She dabbed her mouth with a napkin the way Lola had taught her. "Well, she's been to see Mr. Larry about a tombstone. She brought her baby's ashes from England."

Heather cast a withering glance in Anna Lee's direction. "I'm sorry. I can't talk about it. It's . . . I can't talk about it."

Hilton squeezed her hand. "Of course you can't. We didn't know, Mrs. Rushby. I'm terribly sorry. I can't imagine anything more painful than losing a child."

As soon as they finished dessert, Heather left her chair and kissed Estelle on the cheek. "Thank you for being such a dear, for being so kind to a lonely woman on foreign soil."

Anna Lee had taken all she could for one evening. She knew she risked a switching when she asked, "Don't you have enough money for the trip back home?"

"Anna Lee!" Estelle snapped. Her eyes held a white heat, and she pressed her hand over her heart as though she might faint.

"Well, she said she was lonely."

"Of course she's lonely. I can't believe you could be so rude. Please accept our apologies, Heather."

"No matter, Mrs. Owens . . . Estelle," Heather corrected. "From the mouths of babes . . ." She looked at Anna Lee and smiled, but her eyes were hard as a baby's tombstone.

Anna Lee grimaced. She'd be thirteen next week, had shaved her legs for the first time, and resented being called a baby. Her earliest memories were of measuring her emotions by the number of Prince Albert tobacco cans her dad kept stacked on his chest of drawers. In that moment Heather became a member of a club Anna Lee usually reserved for her mother. *I hate you more than all the Prince Albert cans in the world!*

Hilton thanked Estelle again and escorted Heather to the car.

They were hardly out of earshot when Estelle said, "Well, I never. Talk about eat and run. Even if Anna Lee did insult her, she didn't so much as ask if I needed help with the dishes. Guess they don't have manners in England."

Robert looked up from the cigarette he was rolling. "Why would she, Stelle? She knew Annie was sitting right there in the kitchen waitin' for us to finish up."

"It's just the principle."

"No, you're just not used to having hired help."

"That's the God's truth."

"Well, she would of looked silly offering to go in there with Annie, and you know it. Don't go trying to spoil a nice evening."

"Nice?"

"Yes, nice. Nice that she and Hilton could get acquainted in a proper setting."

"Maybe this is the first 'nice' woman he's ever been interested in."

"You admitting she's nice then?"

"That he thinks so."

"Good God, Estelle, sometimes it makes me tired just trying to talk to you."

"We'll have time for that later, Robert. You won't get tired either because I plan to do most of the talking."

Anna Lee tried to slip away to her room, but Estelle saw her. "And you, Miss Jaundice, can just get out there and help Annie. I was thinking of having a surprise party for your thirteenth birthday, but there won't be any party now. No presents either, and you'll be damn lucky if I make a cake. I've a good mind to switch you right now."

Robert hitched his pants and started out of the room. "That's enough, Estelle."

"For her to bring up a dead baby and then practically tell Heather to go back where she came from."

Robert disappeared around the corner, and she turned back to Anna Lee. "I just can't believe you'd say something like that."

Steely-eyed and angry, Anna Lee wouldn't let Estelle get the best of her. "Well, it's the truth. If she had the money maybe she could go home."

"The truth is that you have no manners."

"The truth is you wouldn't have given me a party anyway."

Robert didn't hear the smack of Estelle's hand on Anna Lee's face. He'd slipped away to the bedroom, pulled his suitcase from under the bed, and felt through the B.V.D.'s he'd left there. He couldn't remember when he'd seen Estelle this worked up. She had to have found the bracelet. He didn't have to decide who it was for any more. He slipped it in his pocket ready to give to Estelle the minute she said something. He wasn't behind the door when the brains were passed out.

Hilton and Heather struggled with conversation until they arrived at the boarding house. He didn't turn off the car and said, "It's early still. Would you like to take a little ride—along the beach maybe?"

Heather turned to him. "Oh, that's ever so nice of you, but I think not. I'm in mourning for my husband you see. And the baby," she added.

"Still? I'm sorry. I hadn't realized that."

"I don't call attention to it by wearing black, but I still mourn in my heart. I feel guilty trying to enjoy myself, you know."

"I'm sure your husband wouldn't want you to feel that way, but I can understand your grief."

She patted his hand and said, "Thank you for understanding. You're a proper chap, and I appreciate that."

Before he realized what was happening, she was out of the car and running up the stairs of the boarding house.

"I'll be damned," Hilton muttered to himself. "I got time though, lady. You can't mourn forever."

Hilton drove around awhile. He was too keyed up with thoughts of the widow Rushby to go home, and seeing Virginia was out. Darrell had returned home from Washington. Finally he drove by Tyler's. Sure enough, there she was in the porch swing. He pulled the car up in front of her house, and she walked over and leaned inside the passenger side window. "Want to come swing a while?"

"Not like you mean," he said.

"I guess not."

"Want to take a little ride then?"

"Give me a minute to tell mother."

What am I doing? I don't want to be with her. He called, "Never mind, I didn't realize it was so late," but she gave no sign of hearing him. He put the car in gear. He'd just leave. But he couldn't do that. The bum evening wasn't her fault. He looked around and there she was, getting in the car.

They rode in silence, and he became exasperated at the effect Heather had on him. When he parked facing the Bay, he grabbed his pipe and left Tyler sitting in the car. He struck a match on the sole of his shoe, and drew the taste of warm tobacco into his lungs. He smoked for a few minutes to calm himself and returned to the car.

"Sorry. I just needed a few minutes alone."

"That's okay. You've had a busy evening. I saw you had a date tonight." Tyler spoke with a forced casualness that wasn't lost on Hilton.

"Not exactly a date. The Owens invited Mrs. Rushby and me to dinner, if you want to call that a date."

"That's what I'd call it. Or a setup. You must've taken her right home though."

"If you're fishing, yes, I did take her right home, and I didn't do this." He couldn't help himself. He pulled Tyler to him, kissing her passionately, clutching her breast. She returned his kisses, stroking the back of his neck, not objecting when his hand moved inside her blouse.

"You don't know how I've longed for you to do that," she whispered against his mouth, her hand sliding toward his crotch.

Her need was like a bucket of cold water on his passion. He pulled his hand from her inside her blouse, and drew a deep breath to slow his breathing. He moved her hand to her lap and pushed her away, the memory of her taut young breast still on the palm of his hand. "Oh, God, Tyler, I'm so sorry. I didn't mean to do that."

"But I wanted you to. You have to know that."

"You're so young. I can't . . ."

"Damn my age! If you'd only give me a chance."

"Tyler, stop. Don't say something we'll both regret. It won't work. I'm sorry. It won't work."

"You're wrong. I know it, but I won't beg. I'm not the begging kind."

"I wouldn't want you to," he said, his voice so quiet she strained to hear what he said. "Don't ever demean yourself that way, not for me or anybody else."

Only the sound of the car starting cut through their silence.

Tyler was back in the porch swing when Larry came walking across the road. He was looking down when he came up the steps without noticing her at first.

"Finish your walk?"

He started, then said, "You been here long?"

"Off and on most of the evening, I guess. The spinster's retreat."

He ignored the remark and said with obvious anger, "I thought I saw Hilton Field's car here earlier."

"He stopped by after his date with Heather."

"His what!"

"His date. The Owens had him and Heather to dinner."

Larry's heart pounded so hard in his ears, he couldn't hear the rest of what Tyler said. It wasn't enough that he had to worry about Tyler, but now Heather too. Worst of all, he realized that if one of them had to be sacrificed to Hilton Fields, he'd rather it be Tyler.

"Dad, are you okay?"

"What? Yeah. I was just remembering some work I left at the shop. I'll be back in a few minutes." He walked through the gate and across the road to his office. He didn't turn on the light. Heather with Hilton. And he'd let it happen. He sat behind his desk trying to stop the shaking that racked his entire body. He couldn't go on like this. He had to find a way to tell Bea they were finished.

Saturday night and Sunday, Larry's hurt and anger seemed more than his body could hold. It was bad enough that Hilton came back from the war unscathed, but that he settled in Bay Harbor was unbearable. Larry had taken an instant dislike to Hilton the first time he met him. A real ladies' man, someone you couldn't trust.

His head felt like it would burst with pain. That Heather would deceive him, not let him know she was going out with Hilton. She'd be waiting for him in the alley, but this was one Sunday night he wouldn't show up. And Tyler, his own Tyler . . .

Larry came to the dinner table Sunday evening with his head bent and his fists clenched against the torment that consumed him. He usually ate in an absentminded way, but this evening he stabbed his food so hard fork made a grating sound when it hit the plate. He chewed rapidly, angrily, the way he acted when he thought about the war. Finally he pushed his chair back and laid his napkin beside his plate.

He raised his hand to his forehead and dropped it. "Tyler," he said a little too loudly, "I will tolerate no tramps in this house."

Beatrice gasped and Tyler's eyes widened. "Dad, what . . ."

Beatrice bristled. "Larry, we've put up with a lot because of what you went through in the war, but I refuse to have you speak to Tyler that way. You should be proud to have such a fine daughter. She's a good girl."

"Oh, you think so? I've seen Hilton Field's car parked out near the cemetery late at night. Now I know who he's out there with. Everybody in town is talking about him and Tyler."

The color drained from Tyler's face. She hadn't been with Hilton at the cemetery late at night.

"See. What did I tell you? She's got guilt written all over her." He failed to notice the pallor on Beatrice's face as well.

Tyler didn't move. She sat in stony silence.

"I don't want you seeing him any more."

"Larry, you can't just ignore your family and then out of the blue come in one night like some drunk barking orders and making rules on the spot. I'll vouch for Tyler."

"I said I . . ." Larry ran from the table, and they could hear him in the bathroom retching.

"At least he has the decency to be sick over that outburst. Tyler, you don't owe me an explanation. I know when you come in at night. We might ask," there was a catch in her voice, "we might ask what Larry was doing in the woods so late himself."

That night the bed shook with Larry's sobs. The two women he loved most in the world had betrayed him, but it was Heather he couldn't live without. He had to ask Beatrice for a divorce. He had to.

Beatrice laid her hand on his shoulder, but he pushed her away. She took her robe from the closet and went out to the porch. There was a breeze, and she listened to the awful scratching sound of magnolia leaves blowing down the street. How many years had it been since she'd sat on this porch with Larry, since they'd done anything together?

She sat in one of the rockers and then got up and walked over to the steps. She pulled her knees up under her chin like a girl. She'd lost enough weight she could do that now, but she wasn't a girl, not any more. Had she ever been? Hadn't she always just been somebody trying to be accepted? She'd tried too hard, she knew that now, perhaps she knew it even then. Maybe that's why she laughed too loud, talked too much, pushed her way into places where she wasn't wanted.

It wasn't until Larry Rose loved her that she believed she had any worth. Larry had made all the difference in her life, and she worshiped him for being able to love her. How had she let him go, let them slip into an everyday existence? They had always been at their best alone, just the two of them. Beatrice was incapable of being her true self when she walked outside the door. She knew Larry recognized that the same as she did and that he'd pitied her for it.

She seemed incapable of changing. It didn't have to be a crowded room. Just one other person and everything was an act. Eventually, she was the act. And there was Tyler, precious Tyler, who was all she worshiped in Larry and what was best in herself.

If it weren't for Tyler, she'd walk into the Bay and not come back. Just walk until the black water swallowed her problems. It was something she thought about more and more often. These weren't unpleasant thoughts for her. Living was. Facing people, keeping up a front. How much longer could she go on? She jumped when Larry touched her shoulder.

"I didn't mean to startle you, but evidently you didn't hear me talking to you."

"What? Oh, yes. I mean, no. No, I didn't hear you. I was lost in thought."

He sat on the steps beside her, and she took the action for tenderness. She laid her hand on his leg and felt him stiffen. She pulled back and clasped her hands between her knees.

"I have to talk to you, Bea. I don't know where to begin, how to say this . . ."

"I know you didn't mean it, Larry. You've had a terrible time since you got home. And if I'm honest, and I'm being honest tonight, I'll have to admit you had somewhat of a terrible time before you left."

"Bea, don't . . ."

"No, don't stop me. I know I've always been a social climber. Couldn't seem to help myself. Maybe that happens when your parents are drunks, and you feel every day of your life you have to live that down. Well, sitting here tonight, I've realized you don't have to be a drunk to ruin someone else's life, to make someone else unhappy."

"Bea, please . . ."

"Let me finish. We always talk about the change in you, but I changed too. I have a pretty good idea you weren't all that happy even before the war."

"Bea, I . . . I don't . . . Bea, we need to reach an understanding. We can't go on this way."

"But, darling, that's what I've been trying to tell you. You really must . . ."

"I'm not your darling!" Larry got up and walked to the front gate before she could finish. He paused there with his back to her. "Don't tell me what to do, Bea. Don't assume authority that isn't yours."

She watched him walk to the funeral home and disappear around back, heard the car start and move into the shadows of the night.

From her bedroom Tyler heard the muffled sounds of her parents' voices and wondered how one house could hold so much pain. First Stephen, and now Hilton.

It seemed impossible that she could love Hilton so desperately and her love not be returned. His nearness, the thought of him was intoxicating. Sitting in his car, she found it nearly impossible keep from touching him. She'd longed to place her hand on the inside of his thigh, but it was a possessive gesture she hadn't dared chance. And then she'd done something so much bolder when he'd held her breast.

If only he would make love to her. Anna Lee told her Hilton wanted children more than anything in the world. If she were carrying his baby, he'd marry her. She knew he would. It wouldn't matter if he didn't love her. She loved him enough for both of them. If he'd make love to her even once she could live on it the rest of her life. But now someone else was living her dream. Who had he been with at the cemetery? She didn't even have the right to ask. No right at all.

CHAPTER
Eighteen

Monday

Every morning at ten o'clock, and every afternoon at three, Horace permitted Heather to break for tea. He'd never allowed that for anyone who worked for him, but Heather's British customs had taken hold in Bay Harbor. Estelle couldn't say she was fond of Heather but realized that instituting tea service at the drugstore would bring a new level of class that even banana splits and her window displays hadn't achieved.

From time to time Virginia Edwards would join Heather. Coffee was the drink of choice in Bay Harbor, but Virginia and a growing number of women began drinking hot tea. They didn't enjoy it as much but liked all that it implied, even in the dead of summer. The elegance achieved at an old black-topped table, overlaid with a white cloth, and set with a tea service, was enough to lure taste buds to the weaker brew.

On Monday morning Virginia and Heather were in the drugstore talking and sipping their Earl Grey when Hilton walked in. When he saw them, his long stride halted mid-step. Their gaze rested just below his chin where he'd left his white dress shirt unbuttoned at the throat, revealing chest hair that was like a dark, thick testament to his virility. Accustomed to admiring looks, Hilton smiled and walked to their table, despising the unease of seeing Heather and Virginia together.

Virginia pushed a chair out and motioned him to sit down.

"Thanks, but I'm here to pick up a prescription for Mother."

"That's too bad. Seems I never see you any more," she said pointedly.

"If Mother didn't need this medicine, wild horses couldn't drag me away. To visit with two such beautiful women . . ." He shrugged. "What can I say?"

"Oh! You do know Heather, don't you, Hilton?"

Hilton looked directly into Heather's silvery gray eyes.

"Yes, I've had that considerable pleasure."

Virginia looked from one to the other, her lower lip in a pout. "Hilton, I'm sure you'll be interested to know that Lola left for her college preparatory school yesterday. She had to go early for orientation." She turned to Heather. "Hilton has always taken such an interest in Lola."

"And I didn't even get to kiss her goodbye! Shame on you for letting her get away like that. Give her my best when you talk to her. Sorry to rush, ladies."

Virginia kept looking over her shoulder toward the pharmacy, but Hilton left by the back door and didn't pass their table again. She turned to Heather. "You never mentioned that you knew Hilton."

"I don't, really. He was in the office one day and —"

Virginia interrupted and smiled broadly, "Oh, you met him at work."

Heather raised her arched brows. "Yes, in the office."

Virginia slipped then and broke her own rule about personal information. "I've known him forever. We met years ago and then have gotten reacquainted here."

"Old friends are the best friends, my mum always said."

"I understand Beatrice Rose had you to dinner recently. Are you two getting to be friends?"

"No, she was just being polite. I haven't seen her since."

"She and Larry make an odd pair. Never could figure out how those two got together. Makes my teeth itch just to look at that man. He's very good looking, don't you think?"

"Yes, I guess you'd say so." Heather looked down and her hand trembled as she lowered her teacup, a pink flush coloring her face. "I'm a working woman so I must be off. Good seeing you, Virginia."

As she walked out the door, Virginia's eyes narrowed and she called quietly, "But you haven't finished your tea."

When Heather returned to the office, she was surprised to see Larry standing at the counter. She hesitated before she walked to her desk and put her purse away. Horace seemed flustered. "Heather, Mr. Rose here needs to check on their payments. He thinks maybe they missed one, and I can't figure out your filing system. Will you take care of him?"

She smiled at Larry. "Oh, I'd be jolly glad to, Mr. Beard." Horace returned to his office, and she asked, "Now, Mr. Rose, what month's bill is concerning you?"

"Pretend you're looking while we talk," he said quietly. "I have to see you tonight."

"I waited for you last night."

"I'm sorry about that. I'd talk right now if I could, but I'll pick you up tonight around ten."

"Here you are, Mr. Rose. Your payments are all up to date," she said loudly. Then, more quietly, "I'll be there." She pressed her hand over his on the counter. He turned his hand palm up under hers, stroking her wrist with his thumb. His mouth was so dry his tongue stuck to the roof of his mouth. *God in heaven, when will I have suffered enough?*

Heather waited in the alley, wearing a dark outfit that made her nearly invisible on this moonless night. When she got in the car he said, "We'll just ride a bit if that's okay with you."

"Just being with you any place is okay with me. After I've come all this way, you jolly well have to know that."

"Foster keeps asking me about the arrangements for the baby. I told him you decided to keep the ashes with you, in an urn. If he ever says anything, that's what you're to say."

"Yes, of course. I'd forgotten he came in that day, but is that all you wanted?" She squeezed his hand.

"No, that isn't all I wanted. Tyler told me about your date with Hilton Fields."

She laughed, "Oh, Larry, darling, I didn't have a date. I'd only seen him in the office once, and when the Owens asked me to dinner, I didn't even know he'd be there. It was a miserable evening, and he took me right home."

Larry let out an audible sigh. "That's a relief. You want to stay away from that guy. He spells trouble. I know Tyler's interested in him, and I'm having problems enough trying to keep her out of his clutches. He's got quite a reputation with the ladies. Women tend to fall all over him, and it has nothing to do with his money."

"Money?"

"Lord yes, he could buy and sell all of us. You ever see his mother's house?"

"I don't know. Where is it?"

"Across the highway facing the Bay, the house with white pillars and a pink tile roof."

"That's his mother's home? It's beautiful. I've often admired it."

"Yep. She's well fixed too."

"I had no idea."

"Just watch out for him. He's smooth. I see his car parked different places at night. He's got a woman, and I was afraid it was Tyler. Now I'm thinking maybe it's somebody else. I'd love to find out who, but he's cagey."

"Sounds like he needs to be. He came in while Virginia and I were in the drugstore today, and . . ."

"Just so long as it isn't you he's with."

"It isn't me, darling, you can be sure of that, but you're pretty cagey yourself, you know."

Larry grinned. "Never thought of it that way. I better take you home now. I told Beatrice I was going to the shop."

"Larry, how long are we . . ."

"I know. I just need a little more time. Soon now."

Heather sighed. "That's becoming a familiar refrain, isn't it?"

"I know. I'm sorry. It's just so hard. I don't love Beatrice any more. You know that. I guess guilt's thicker than love."

"I feel bad sometimes that I don't have any guilt. Beatrice is pitiful, truly she is, but I can't feel guilty for loving you. I just can't."

"Don't worry about it. I have enough guilt for both of us."

By Tuesday morning Tyler had relived her passionate evening with Hilton hundreds of times and woke with fresh hope that something serious might develop between them. If he didn't feel something for her, how could he have been so overcome with desire? She didn't care how much Larry disapproved of him. She'd lost her real father somewhere in France.

With Hilton's desperate need for children, all she had to do was arouse his passion again, and maybe, just maybe . . .

She knew he went to the post office every day around three, and Tyler made it a point to be there as often as she could. She pretended that she still looked for word from Stephen, even though she could hardly remember him at times, so strong was Hilton's influence over her emotions. And no, she told herself, what she felt was much more than rebound. When she thought of Stephen, she saw only the framed picture in the drawer of her nightstand.

Dog days were drawing to a close, but summer still burned hot. Tyler wanted to look cool and refreshed so she dressed carefully in a green and pink floral print pinafore and barefoot sandals. She brushed her shoulder length pageboy until it made a luminous backdrop for the cultured pearls Stephen had fastened around her neck. Despite all that had happened, she couldn't remove the pearls. Stephen's hands had placed them there.

Tyler was lingering over the photographs of criminals posted on the walls of the post office when Hilton came up behind her and laughed.

"Looking for someone you know?"

"Actually, I was looking for you," she replied.

"Touché. But despite what you might think, I'm not a criminal, Miss Rose."

"Oh, I didn't mean . . ."

She was interrupted when Heather came in the post office. Hilton saw her and turned away from Tyler.

"Mrs. Rushby."

"Mr. Fields." She smiled. "But please, my friends call me Heather."

"I'd be delighted to count myself among your friends," he gave a slight pause and said softly, "Heather."

She turned away and walked to the bank of mailboxes that stretched the length of the back wall.

Tyler said, "Hilton, even the children call her Heather. That's no big deal."

"It is to me. Nice seeing you, Tyler."

He left Tyler numb with hurt. Her crisp dress had wilted, and she felt uncomfortably warm. She turned and watched him follow Heather to the mailboxes. Only the slight narrowing of her eyes betrayed her anger.

Heather knelt to work the combination of the large Florida Power box close to the floor. Hilton leaned over talking to her, so close she nearly knocked him over when she stood up. Heather slid the mail into a large envelope and walked past Tyler, giving a brief nod.

Hilton walked toward Tyler, snapped his fingers, turned and went back for his mother's mail. When he passed her on the way out he said only, "She's out of mourning."

If Heather hadn't known it at three o'clock that Tuesday, by five it was evident Hilton was a man in a hurry. When she got off work, he was standing on the sidewalk waiting for her.

"Could I give you a ride?"

Heather raised one eyebrow and smiled. "Have you forgotten that I live but a block from here?"

"Certainly not, but I know the long way home."

"I'm always eager to learn something new."

When Hilton opened the door of his blue Pontiac coup, Heather slid onto the seat, and pulled her long, shapely legs inside with one deft movement.

He drove to the beach highway and didn't stop until they'd reached Panama City. Neither of them spoke until he parked in front of a popular seafood restaurant. "I like a woman who is comfortable with silence."

"I'm not much of a talker. Used to drive my mum batty."

"Well, it doesn't bother me a bit. I think we'll get along just fine."

Heather smiled. "That's nice to know."

They had dinner and were back by nine o'clock. He walked Heather as far as the swinging doors that were midway up the stairs to the boarding house. She stood close to him, and he was about to kiss her when one of the boarders started down the stairs toward them.

Heather placed her palm on his cheek for a brief moment and then turned and continued up the stairs. He grasped the swinging door to keep it from closing and didn't take his eyes off her. When she reached the landing, she turned and blew him a kiss.

The next morning at ten o'clock Hilton was back in the drugstore. He ordered two cups of tea and sat watching the door for Heather. A few moments later Virginia came in.

"Why, Hilton, how thoughtful." Virginia sat down, helped herself to some tea, and stirred sugar into one of the cups. He was sliding his cup in front of the empty chair when Heather came in. He stood and pulled the chair out for her.

"My goodness, it's just like a tea party, isn't it?" Virginia asked.

"I hadn't intended it to be a party. I was waiting for Heather."

Virginia drew a sharp breath. "Forgive me for intruding then." She stood and walked out the door without saying a word.

"I hope you don't mind, Heather."

She took the chair he held out and placed her hand on top of his. "I don't mind at all. You really are thoughtful, you know."

Hilton raised his eyebrows and smiled. "You'd be amazed just how thoughtful I can be."

That afternoon Hilton was in the drugstore again at three when Heather came for her tea, and at five he waited outside the Florida Power Company. By Friday night when Heather usually met Larry, they'd been together part of every day and every night. He didn't pry into her past, ask about her husband. They each confided what they wanted the other to know. He asked only one question, apologizing before she had any inkling of what he was about to say.

They were in his car parked in one of the cuts at the beach. He took her hand in his and kissed her palm. "I don't quite know how to say this, Heather, except that it means all the world to me. I want you to know that. And if you weren't important to me, I'd never dream of being so personal, so forward. I . . . I . . ."

"Hilton, stop. It's okay. In the short while we've known each other, I hope you realize we've made a connection of sorts. Speak freely to me. I mean it. I'm a big girl, and I'm not easily offended."

"The last thing I'd ever want to do is offend you, but this touches on a painful subject. I know you've had a child, and I know a child lost can never be replaced, but would you . . . I mean do you want . . . do you plan to have other children?"

Heather lifted his fingers to her lips and kissed them. "Not by myself, I can't."

He pushed her backward on the seat, his hand cupping her breast. His tongue explored her mouth with wide sweeps and then a steady pulsing, in and out over her lips until she cried out with desire.

Larry waited for Heather in the alley like he did every Friday night, but she never came. He drove to the cemetery and then back to town. A sense of impending disaster overwhelmed him. He knew he couldn't wait any longer to talk to Beatrice. He started home with every intention of asking her for a divorce.

When he reached his house, a dozen or more cars were parked along the street. The police car was at the funeral home and every light blazed.

Anna Lee stood behind the porch railing at the funeral home and watched Larry get out of his car and cross the street, walk past the swinging sign, and up the steps.

He clenched his fists to keep his hands from shaking. Heather always waited for him in the alley. She hadn't been there so something had to have happened to her. He looked down and saw dried blood on the floor of the porch, knew it had to be Heather's. What in God's name had happened?

The Chief of Police walked up and gripped Larry's shoulder. "We're glad you're here. We didn't know where you were."

There was such a roaring in his head he could hardly think. He grabbed Buster by the shoulders and shouted, "Where is she? Was she in an accident?"

Buster backed away. "Mary's inside with Foster."

"But where's Heather?"

"Who?"

"Heather!"

"How the hell would I know?" Buster went to the edge of the porch and spit.

Anna Lee walked over and took Larry's hand, touching it to her wet cheek. "Mr. Larry," she pulled him to one side. "It isn't Heather, Mr. Larry."

"Thank God. What happened?"

"It's T. J. He's dead."

"What?"

The chief walked back to them. "It's your nephew. A hit and run. He was riding his bicycle on the beach road."

Anna Lee broke in. "When he didn't come to supper, Mr. Foster came to my house looking for him."

Buster attempted to hitch his pants up over his fat gut. "Anna Lee, maybe you better go on home now. I need to talk to Larry."

He was the Chief of Police, but Anna Lee didn't leave. She stepped back into the shadows and listened.

"It was a drunk, Larry. We caught him, but not before Foster saw his boy. Handlebar went clear through his stomach. Foster wouldn't let us touch him. Picked him up and walked home with him calling to Mary, saying over and over, 'Mary, T. J.'s been hurt.' He was hurt all right. Poor little bugger."

Beatrice came out to the porch and embraced Larry. "It's so awful. Dr. Mason sedated Mary, but see if you can do something for Foster. He needs you."

Larry walked inside on wooden legs. His body had lost all feeling.

CHAPTER
Nineteen

Saturday, August 31

Bay Harbor became a place of mourning. The funeral home was filled all hours of the day with good people trying to help and comfort, but they were horrified when Foster insisted on embalming his own child. Mary had bathed him, touching his stilled body more gently than she'd ever done in life. She heard Foster cry out once from the prep room, but he'd locked the door and she couldn't go to him.

Larry stayed in his office, sheet after sheet of paper crumpled on the floor, available if Foster needed him. Anna Lee stopped by with a thermos of coffee and smoothed one of the sheets of paper.

"I guess it's hard to capture someone like T. J., Mr. Larry. He was never still long enough."

"That's true, but I feel guilty. I didn't know my own nephew. I never thought I'd need to, not for this anyway." He waved his arm across his desk.

"I knew him, Mr. Larry. We were sort of best friends. I can tell you how I knew T. J. if you want."

"Then I need your help. Please . . . "

"T. J. was so many things, but I guess he was best known for his death tours."

"Death tours? Death tours! What in God's name are you talking about?"

"Let me pour you a cup of coffee. I can't draw the picture, but I can tell you so you can know T. J. a little better, good enough for a life drawing, maybe."

She got the cups and poured two cups of coffee. She pulled the chair, the one Heather always sat in, around the desk, and they sat knee to knee. She spoke quietly, reverently, shaping words into the life of a skinny, freckled faced boy.

"Death tours were T. J.'s invention. He became a sort of leader, taking us on those tours. He made sure we knew he was an authority, and we never doubted him. The best death tours . . ."

In the end they both cried, but Larry shed tears from the depth of his soul, tears not just for T. J.'s life but his own.

The Methodist Church where they held T. J.'s funeral was a barn like structure of un-insulated bead board that lacked the grandeur of the funeral home; but T. J. had been christened there, and it was where he attended Sunday school when he could be persuaded to go. His parents felt it only fitting he should end there.

The maple casket with brass fittings was placed at the front of the church, below the pulpit. A spray of white orchids covered one end of the casket. The stained glass windows, so out of place in the gaunt sanctuary, were lined front to back with baskets of white lilies and carnations. The church was nearly suffocating with the odor, but the flowers softened somewhat the sharp deck-of-card faces of the stained glass saints.

The church filled to overflowing with sorrowful friends and relatives. Even Heather was there. She hadn't really known T. J., but for a time Larry's family had been hers as well. At least in her own mind. After all, she'd given up everything for Larry—her family, her country. *Be honest, Heather. You're in church. Okay, so it wasn't much to give up, and she'd expected to have a better life in the states anyway. What a joke that turned out to be. Little wonder Hilton, with his smooth ways and easy money, could make her wonder if she'd ever really loved Larry.*

There was a stirring among the mourners, and Heather's thoughts returned to T. J.

The children began arriving and filled three long pews. They wore Sunday clothes. The boys had slicked down hair while the girls' was festooned with ribbons. People marveled at their manners. Not one of them turned to look back and see who was coming in the church. They didn't whisper among themselves or fidget. T. J. had taught them well.

People gasped when a pigeon flew from the bell tower and over the congregation before circling and flying out the open door. The children craned their necks toward the casket. That had been a favored trick of T. J.'s, another one his parents hadn't known about. He'd slip out from his Sunday school class and frighten the birds in the tower so they'd fly into the church.

Anna Lee felt numb, had trouble believing why she was there. She listened as a young schoolteacher with a sweet, clear soprano began singing *Whispering Hope*. That brought her out of her stupor. *Whispering Hope* for T. J.? *Amazing Grace* was the rousing kind of song that should send T. J. on his journey. *How sweet the sound that saved a wretch like me* . . . T. J. would have liked that. He'd never mind being a wretch.

Anna Lee heard movement and saw an usher standing at the end of their pew directing them to go forward past the open casket. When it was her turn to look, her lips began to quiver. He was so still. She couldn't just leave him there like that. She reached her hand inside the casket and linked her pinky finger around his cold, stiff one. That's when she accepted he was really dead. She was about to run when something caught her eye. Someone had dropped a dime on the lapel of T. J.'s dark blue suit. *Oh, T. J.* . . .

Bay Harbor didn't often lose its children. People knew they'd never forget T. J's terrible death, the loss of one so young, but life did go on. Two months had passed, and October came with merest hint of fall in the air. Pieces shifted and changed, but life kept its pace, better for some than others.

Heather and Hilton never broke stride, became a familiar sight in Bay

Harbor. Beatrice Rose couldn't understand why that made her so happy, but it did. Heather often joined Hilton at his nearly completed home. Rubbing salt in his wound, Larry walked along the beach looking up at the house on the bluff, or hill as Hilton called it, often catching sight of Heather standing in the front yard, Hilton's arm around her waist, the wind whipping her skirt close to her body.

How had he let this happen! And yet he had let it happen, despite the passionate arguments, Heather's pleading, her tears. She warned him. She begged him to ask for a divorce. He didn't know why he couldn't. He wanted it with every fiber of his being. Heather was all he'd ever wanted in life. Was giving up Heather part of what he'd promised God on Omaha Beach?

Heather was no longer a stranger in Mrs. Richard's home and frequently accompanied him to the Owens' as well. They weren't unaware of the countless pairs of eyes watching them, Larry's and Tyler's, especially. Tyler thought she'd die, prayed she'd die, and Virginia Edwards just wanted to hurt someone. She knew she had no rights, no legal rights to Hilton, but she felt bound to him in ways he couldn't begin to understand. There were no more nights on the beach, no sighs in the back seat of Hilton's car. She was just a frustrated housewife once more. She held a trump card but she couldn't use it.

Hilton and Heather made frequent trips out of town to select furniture for the house. They spent hours in distant towns searching bookstores, choosing books for the library Hilton designed. "For once I'm going to please my mother," Hilton confided to Heather. And while they traveled, tongues wagged, but Heather was so sweet and innocent, it was hard to imagine there was any impropriety. And after all, her stomach remained perfectly flat.

Larry was no stranger to suffering, but without Heather his life became a bloody beach of torment. He couldn't believe it was too late for them. Heather still loved him. She told him so in a letter he found on his pillow at the shack.

They could move away. He'd practice law again. God didn't enter into it. They'd have the life he'd dreamed of. He had the courage now. His mind was made up. This was the night he'd ask Beatrice for a divorce. Nothing would stop him this time. He left the shop early and went home to change before dinner. When he walked past Tyler's room, he saw her sitting on the floor at the foot of her bed. Her face was swollen from crying, and she was bent, like a broken doll. He knelt beside her. "What's happened? Is there word from Stephen?"

She looked up and didn't say anything for several minutes. "Daddy, are you okay? You know Stephen was declared dead."

"That's right. I remember now. I'm sorry, baby. I've had a rough day. I forgot." He tried to put his arm around her, but she pulled away.

"What's wrong then? You got a problem you need to discuss?" Guilt weighed on him because his real fear was that she might prevent him from settling the task he'd set for himself.

"No, nothing like that."

He clenched his fists trying to conceal his anxiety and forced himself to show some concern. "Would you like me to call your mother to come talk to you?"

"No! I don't want to talk to anyone."

He kissed her cheek and started toward the door.

"Heather and Hilton are married."

He didn't move. He couldn't even turn to look at her or ask how she knew. He waited and finally she spoke again.

"Anna Lee told me. They were on one of their buying trips and called Anna Lee's parents to join them. Robert and Estelle Owens were their only attendants. Mrs. Richards will have a big reception for them when they get back." She gave a bitter laugh. "And that's all the news I have for now."

Larry still couldn't move, and Tyler did nothing to make it easier for him. The front door slammed and Beatrice walked down the hall. She stopped at Tyler's door, frightened by the tableau of grief evident in the postures of her daughter and husband, never guessing she had been spared.

Until the night of the wedding reception, Estelle had never been inside Mrs. Richards' house. She couldn't have been more nervous had she been going to Buckingham Palace.

"Now, Robert, I hope you don't go calling Mrs. Richards by her first husband's name."

"Well, if I do, she don't care."

"Of course she cares. That isn't her name!"

"What if it ain't. She knows who I mean. She's alus been Miz Fields to me. I've known her longer than anybody in Bay Harbor. I knew her when that silver hair was auburn."

"That doesn't change a thing. If you want people to think you're ignorant, just go ahead. There's no reasoning with you. Amy and Johnn will be there, and you won't hear them calling her Mrs. Fields."

"That's their business what they call her, Estelle. Just don't forget that house will be ours some day no matter what we call Hilton's mother. Remember that."

"You think I haven't? If only Amy knew. Oh, how I'd love to tell her." Estelle held her arm up to admire the gold bracelet Robert had given her.

"We're not telling nobody. I gave Hil my word."

"I know, but it's hard at times. Here, let me straighten your tie. And hold your shoulders up."

Anna Lee was sullen, her eyes were swollen from crying. She hadn't been invited to the reception, and she knew it wasn't Hilton's fault. He confided to her that Heather didn't want to hurt anyone's feelings, and if Anna Lee were invited, they'd have to ask a multitude of children. Anna Lee didn't blame Hilton for believing Heather. He didn't know her like she did.

Estelle looked back over her shoulder as they walked out the door.

"I'm sorry, Anna Lee. Maybe this will teach you not to be smart-mouthed with people."

I hate you more than all the . . .

There was a small receiving line when they walked in the door. Mrs. Richards, Hilton and Heather.

Mrs. Richards' was elegant in a full length crepe dress of old rose. Her silver hair was caught up in back with an elaborate rhinestone comb. She kissed Robert on the cheek and embraced Estelle who whispered, "You look like a bride yourself, Mrs. Richards."

Heather and Hilton were the perfect wedding cake ornament. He was every inch the groom in a white dinner jacket and aqua cummerbund designed to match the bride's floor length silk dress. Later they cut a wedding cake of the same color. With one arm around Heather's waist, Hilton began making toasts. He made three.

He toasted Heather and then all the friends who were there to celebrate with them. His final toast was his most emotional. He raised his glass and said, "Mrs. Fields and I," he turned and kissed Heather on the cheek, "hope that you will be in our home for another celebration about. . . what would you say, darling, a year from now?" He raised his glass higher. "To our firstborn child. In the meantime, come visit us. Come see the nursery that awaits our baby, the beginning of our family." When he kissed Heather a second time, she blushed with a look of innocence.

Someone said that as best man, Robert should say a few words. Robert choked on his champagne and Estelle grabbed his cup and plate before he spilled something on the oriental carpet. She closed her eyes briefly and prayed. Robert shouldn't have had anything to drink. She looked around for Johnn to see if he could help him out, but Johnn just waved and smiled.

Robert cleared his throat and looked at Hilton. "I ain't never been much with words. Hilton knows that, and he knows nobody here wishes him and Heather more happiness than I do. I couldn't care more for him if he was my own kin, and that's the God's truth." He took his handkerchief and wiped his eyes, and everyone started applauding. He opened his mouth to continue, and Estelle hissed, "You're done, Dale Carnegie, just relax."

Estelle tucked a napkin in her purse to take to Anna Lee as a souvenir. Heather and Hilton were printed on it in silver and below their names, October 27, 1946.

The champagne made Robert so dizzy Estelle had to drive home, another humiliation. People smiled as she helped Robert get in the car. She slammed his door, squared her shoulders and walked to the driver's side with a measure of dignity suited to someone who would one day live in a house with white columns and a pink tile roof.

Estelle recognized the true distance between the Owens' home and Mrs. Richards', but in miles it was only a short drive for her to navigate. For that she was grateful. She was nearly as dizzy as Robert, but it had nothing to do with alcohol.

Mrs. Richards' house was even more beautiful than she could have imagined. She wondered if they'd get any of the furniture. As exciting as it was to contemplate, she felt bad for anticipating Mrs. Richards' demise. Still, she couldn't help but wonder if Hilton would want Larry Rose to do a life scene for his mother.

When they got home, Robert rushed to the bedroom to lie down.

Estelle walked over to bed and slipped his shoes off. "Why, Robert, I just realized none of the Rose family was there. Don't you think that's kinda funny?"

Estelle walked to the dresser and unscrewed the backs of her earrings. She looked at Robert's reflection in the mirror.

"They wasn't there?"

"No, they weren't. Considering they had Heather over to eat and all, they must have been invited. I'm just surprised none of them made an appearance."

"Oh well, darling, only the Shadow knows," Robert quoted from the popular radio program and started laughing.

"Robert Owens, you're drunk. You ought to be ashamed. At your best friend's wedding reception."

"Can you think of a better place? I sure as hell cain't. Hil don't care. He's so happy to be married, he ain't seeing nothing but Heather. God it makes me glad to see him so happy."

"I thought Heather looked kinda peaked, didn't you? That was a stunning dress, but she still looked peaked."

"They was just back from their honeymoon. She probably didn't get a lot of sleep." Robert laughed. "Maybe there's a baby on the way. That'd sure make Hil happy. Cain't get over how much he wants a family."

"That's a wonder all right. It wouldn't surprise me if he had a few young'uns scattered across the country already."

"There you go putting Hil down again after all he's done for us. You're one ungrateful woman, Estelle."

"I'm not ungrateful. I'm just realistic. You never see things clearly where Hilton's concerned. You think he's so perfect."

"Maybe not perfect, but close. And he'll always be my best friend," Robert answered lazily and yawned.

"Why, Robert Owens! It seems to me sometimes you think more of Hilton than you do your own family. And speaking of family, did you feel the chill between Mrs. Richards and Heather? Mrs. Richards didn't seem as happy as I'd thought she'd be over this turn of events. Something's not right there. Don't you agree? Robert?" He didn't answer and she looked at the reflection of his slack mouth in the mirror. Dale Carnegie was sound asleep.

CHAPTER
Twenty

January 1947

Another year distanced Bay Harbor from the war, but it distanced the
Rose family from each other. Larry, Beatrice and Tyler remained in
a state of trauma, each of them trying to form new alliances, searching to
find new ways to get by in the world.

Larry had come to hate Beatrice. He knew it wasn't her fault, that she
had nothing to do with it, but all the malice he might have felt toward
Heather was directed at Beatrice instead. He resented her for being so
much older, for being so plain, for trapping him into marriage. Foster had
known what he was talking about. She had trapped him all right. Larry
wanted her to suffer in his presence the way he suffered in Heather's. He
sat at his desk devising ways to make her unhappy.

He no longer shared their bed. He stayed at his office or slept on the
sofa. He took his meals at the boarding house and had a toaster and coffee pot in his office at the funeral home. He and Foster spent long hours
there together. Foster was a broken man. They were broken men.

Alone in her own world, Tyler grew more and more reclusive. Determined to build a wall no one could penetrate, she built it of cold indiffer-
ence, of barbed words, and failed love. But she found that no wall could
shut out the pain of seeing Hilton and Heather together. She was ever
watchful in her effort to avoid them until one day she saw them from
across the street as they were coming out of the drugstore. Her knees

buckled and she fainted dead away on the sidewalk.

Hilton and Heather got in their car and drove away without a glance at all the people trying to revive Tyler.

Beatrice had finally accepted that they weren't a family any more. They hadn't been a family since Larry returned from the war. *Returned?* Had he ever really returned? If he had, he brought the war home with him.

They moved about in their own space, never touching, going about like ghosts in the dark, unfriendly house. Beatrice, in her one act of defiance, applied for the job Heather had held at the Florida Power Company.

Beatrice and Horace had known each other in high school so they were comfortable together. She often thought she should give him a shave every day at noon and save him the trip home. She smiled at the thought. Beatrice could smile at any number of things.

It might have been small comfort to the Rose family but by June of 1947, smiles were no longer so abundant at the home of Mr. and Mrs. Hilton Fields. A framed picture of Heather and Hilton taken the night of their wedding reception had a place of honor on the Owens' living room wall. A more recent picture would not have captured the air of happiness evident in the bridal couple. They'd been married eight months with no sign of a baby on the way.

"Poor Hilton," became Robert Owens' mournful refrain. "God in heaven, how that boy wants a baby. Never saw anything like it."

Estelle never forgot that she'd hadn't borne a child and said, "Well, I feel sorry for Heather. It isn't all about Hilton. Everybody in town is just waiting for her to start bursting out of her dresses."

"Hilton most of all though. I never seen him so frustrated in my life."

"At least he's rich. To be poor and frustrated would be worse."

"Hil would give ever cent he's got to have a young'un. Hope he'll have one before too much longer."

"That nursery they furnished is collecting dust. I think that was a mistake. It's a constant reminder, almost like a death in the family. There's even baby clothes hanging in the closet."

"Yeah, Hil showed me all that stuff. He don't talk about it so much any more. You can see the pain in his face."

"Talking of pain, have you seen Larry Rose lately? He looks terrible. Those two brothers, both of 'em look awful. Poor T. J. That really shook Anna Lee."

"I notice she ain't asking for a bicycle any more."

"No, I doubt she'll ever want a bicycle now."

Anna Lee was in the bathroom painting her toenails, wondering if Lola would say she was too young yet. She missed Lola, even her criticism.

She sat on the floor with her back to the door so she could eavesdrop on her parents' conversation. No, she surely didn't want a bicycle. She'd gone to the Western Auto store and pressed the handlebar of a bike hard against her stomach. *How had it felt to T. J.? He'd become his own death tour.*

And she didn't feel one bit sorry for Heather. She'd asked Mr. Larry once what happened to the baby's ashes, and he said Heather had them in an urn. When she asked Heather where she kept the urn, for a minute she acted like she didn't know what Anna Lee was talking about. Then she told her she was a spiteful child, and it was none of her business. She hadn't acted a bit sad. Anna Lee wondered if there had ever been a baby. The only person who acted sad in that house was Hilton.

He'd be even sadder if he knew about her and Mr. Larry. I'd like to be spiteful and tell him, but I wouldn't hurt Hilton to get back at Heather. I don't think I would anyway.

A winding road across from the Bay followed an incline to the Fields' home. A sprawling one floor dwelling, it would come to be called a modified ranch. Painted white with dark blue shutters, it gleamed in the morning sun. The elevation was protection from a possible storm surge and provided an ample view to people passing on the highway. A generous porch stretching the width of the house was decorated with white columns, and floor to ceiling windows banked the ornate molding around the front door. No detail had been overlooked, except perhaps the choice of occupants.

With Robert handling the majority of Hilton's business, he was free to spend most of his time home with Heather, working on a baby, he'd told Robert. Heather had escaped her cell at the boarding house but still felt like a prisoner, physically and mentally. There were days when she actually felt nostalgic about Larry's shack in the woods. She'd slipped away one afternoon and gone there, almost hoping she'd run into Larry. She was relieved she hadn't. She had too much to lose if Hilton ever found out about them.

If only Hilton would forget about children. They could be so happy together if everything didn't center around getting her pregnant. She was bored. Bored with Hilton, bored with talk of children. Conversations with Hilton were tense, frequently leading to arguments.

"Hilton, let's forget about having a family for now. Next month it'll be your American holiday, 4th of July. Let's throw a big party."

"Don't change the subject, Heather. I don't want a party. Don't you understand we aren't youngsters any more?" Hilton reasoned with Heather. "Maybe we should see a doctor," he offered, not for the first time.

"Hilton, if anyone needs to see a doctor, it's you. I had a child. Remember?"

"Yes, but . . ."

"But what? Hilton, we have a beautiful home and can have a wonderful life if we never have children. Lots of people don't have children."

"We aren't lots of people, Heather."

"Maybe not, but I get sick and tired of your blaming me."

"I'm not blaming you. I just think we should see a doctor. I'd like to find a specialist, in Atlanta maybe."

"Well don't forget that I had a child and could have another easy enough. I feel like a fool with that nursery decorated upstairs. It's almost as bad as the library with all those fancy books you never read. The only thing that'll ever occupy that nursery is dust. Dust, Hilton, dust! You are the problem, sir, not me. You're the ladies' man. Maybe you wore yourself out before you married me. Did you ever think of that? Just because you fancy yourself this great lover . . ."

Heather stopped when she saw the look on Hilton's face. She didn't mistake the shock in his eyes or the pallor of his skin. A huge vein throbbed in his temple, and he thrust his trembling hands in his pockets. *Oh, I shouldn't have said those hurtful things, but I've held it in all this time, being sweet, nice Heather. I'm so sick of it!* She took a deep breath and lifted her hand to stroke his face. He struck it so hard she winced with pain.

He walked past her and out the front door. She hadn't moved when she heard him fall. She ran to the porch and saw him lying at the foot of the front steps, bleeding from the blow to his head. She stood for several minutes and then slowly, carefully walked down the stairs. She felt a faint pulse and then went inside and called Larry. He was in his office, nearly speechless that she'd called him.

"For God's sake, Heather, I know you're in shock, but get a doctor. He could die."

"I'm just so frightened, Larry. We had a terrible quarrel. I said hurtful things he'll never forgive me for."

"Never mind. I'll get a doctor for you. Go make him comfortable."

She hung up then and went to the bathroom where she ran cold water over a towel. She walked back down the steps, noting that Hilton hadn't moved. She sat on the bottom step and cradled his head in her lap, trying to clean the blood from his forehead. Such was the touching scene when Dr. Mason arrived. Heather shed her first tears.

Her thoughts darted. Would Hilton ever forgive her? She'd shown a side of herself he'd never seen, become someone he'd never known. Could she make him believe it was only the stress of wanting a child as much as he did?

"Mrs. Fields!" Heather jumped.

"You must get hold of yourself. He has to be hospitalized immediately. I've called an ambulance."

"But he just hit his head . . ."

"It's more than that, Mrs. Fields. Much more."

Anna Lee was on the way to her Uncle John's house when the

screaming ambulance sped past. She didn't know it might as well have been for her.

Heather insisted on riding in the ambulance with Hilton. The screaming sirens were nothing compared to the wailing inside her head. She'd heard sirens before, plenty of them during the war, but these sirens were her doing. She couldn't believe what she'd done. She was as worried that she'd endangered her marriage as she was about the state of her husband's health.

Dr. Mason was right. It was much more than a simple fall. Hilton suffered from a cerebral embolism. He was in a coma. When this news was given to Heather, standing there with Hilton's mother, she had to be sedated to stop the shaking.

It was Mrs. Richards who went to her son's room and held his hand, speaking to him softly, saying words of comfort. When Robert came in she looked up and said, "I don't know if he can hear me or not, but I have to pray he can." Robert nodded and walked to the other side of the bed. Hot tears fell unashamedly on Hilton's hand.

Heather never mentioned the argument. Larry was the only one who knew. She told everyone Hilton was just going out for some Coca Colas. Oh, she'd never forgive herself for having forgotten to buy them. She knew he loved them so. But he hadn't blamed her. He was so forgiving, so loving that way. He told her he'd get them and be right back. "Right back," she said and her voice broke. Every time.

What the nurses couldn't get over was the grief of Robert Owens. "Why that man talks to Mr. Fields till he's hoarse." The head nurse swore she heard him crying. They'd never seen anything like it, not from a grown man.

One of the doctors heard them talking and looked up from his clipboard. "That banty rooster cry? I doubt it. Not Robert Owens!"

"Hello?"

"Larry?" The voice was little more than a whisper.

"Hello? I can't hear you."

She cleared her throat and said, "Larry, it's Heather." He didn't answer and she went on. "I need to talk to you. I think I'll lose my mind if I don't talk to somebody."

"I don't really think that's my place now, do you?"

"Oh, darling, I know it isn't. I can't blame you for hating me, but please. I need you so."

"I never stopped needing you."

"Larry, don't . . . I'm so alone. Could we — could we meet at your hideout?"

"Heather, do you know what you're risking?"

"Larry, you were always a risk."

"I guess I was. Okay. I'll meet you at the edge of the woods tonight at ten o'clock."

"I'll be waiting."

<hr />

Bay Harbor was a town of good people, and they all wanted to help. They went and talked, hoping Hilton would hear, hoping to raise some spark to give him the will to live, but as the weeks turned into months, the spark began to fade.

Tyler thought she could revive the spark, that there might be a chance for her and Hilton yet. It was her only hope. She held Hilton's hand and leaned close to his ear, whispering her secret, but there was no change.

Virginia Edwards was another surprise for the nurses. She visited regularly and seemed nearly as grief-stricken as Mr. Field's own wife. They were there together sometimes, talking to Hilton and to each other.

Tyler went to see Hilton only once more. Since her secret hadn't had the desired effect, she asked to be left alone, and closed the door. There wasn't a lot that surprised the nurses any more.

Tyler slipped into the bed beside Hilton, placing his hand on her breast. "I didn't mean to hurt you, Hilton. I only told you what I'd learned in hopes of giving you the will to live, to get your life back on track. I never meant to make things worse for you. I wanted to give you hope for something better. Oh, Hilton, if only you'd loved me." She poured her heart out, sharing her pent-up emotions.

She told him about the life she'd dreamed of for the two of them, told him how much she loved him, "but, Hilton," she said with tears in her voice, "you were only heat lightning for me, and I needed a local storm. But if you'll just get well, I'll be content with heat lightning for the rest of my life." She pressed his hand hard against her bare breast. "I promise."

Deep in thought, Tyler closed the door to Hilton's room and made her way down the corridor of the hospital. She walked slowly, her head bowed. One of the nurses whispered, "You spose she's praying?"

Another nurse pointed toward the door. "If she was, she's not any more."

Tyler stopped just outside the entrance to the hospital, squared her shoulders, lifted her chin, and resumed the purposeful stride that had been so typical of Tyler Rose.

In no time she was walking through the door of the Florida Power Company. Beatrice came out of Horace's office when she heard the door slam. Tyler noticed how nice she looked. There was a faint blush to her cheeks and her hair was in some disarray, giving her a softer look. Tyler started to compliment her, but thought better of it and blurted out her message. "I'm going to Guam!" That's all she said before she turned and walked out the door.

Beatrice gasped a small, "Oh," turned around and saw Horace standing close behind her. The last thing she noticed before she passed out was the shadow of a beard on his face. She grabbed for his arms and took him down with her.

It was the only time in Horace's life a woman had ever lain on top of him, and even if she was unconscious, he found it a pleasing sensation.

Hilton had been in a coma for three months when Virginia Edwards went in one night long after visiting hours. She knew Clara, the nurse on duty. She had a daughter Lola's age and let Virginia go inside and close the door. Clara looked at the other nurses and shrugged her shoulders.

For several minutes Virginia sat on the side of the bed holding Hilton's hand. Finally she raised his hand to her lips and kissed each of his fingers. "I hope you can hear me, Hilton, because I'm going to tell you a secret. When you're well, if you don't want to keep it a secret, well, I'll live with that. But this is my gift to you.

"You have a daughter, darling. Lola is yours. That's why I was afraid for you to be around her, why I had to rush her off to school. I was scared. I was afraid you might think back to our long ago night together and figure things out." Virginia laughed softly, "When she was born I was terrified she might have white hair. She does have your eyes and slender build.

"Darrell couldn't love her more. He thinks she's his daughter, but she's yours. Always was." She wiped her eyes. "I wish I'd told you before but I was afraid. I hope you'll forgive me." She leaned over and kissed his cheek.

For a minute she thought she saw his eyelids flutter. Then Clara came in and Virginia started for the door, wondering if she'd only imagined it. She felt a chill and shivered, turning to look back.

Clara shook her head. "He's gone."

Forgetting that Lola had taught her to walk slowly and sway her hips, Anna Lee ran home from Tyler's the same as she had when she was only eleven or twelve. She tried swinging her hips as she ran, but it only slowed her down. "Mama! Mama!"

Estelle stood in the middle of the living room, a stunned look on her face.

Disappointed that she might not be the one to give her the news, Anna Lee asked, "You know already, don't you?"

Estelle nodded.

"I can't believe it. Who would ever have thought Tyler would go to Guam looking for Stephen?"

"What? What are you talking about?"

"You said you'd heard. Tyler's going to Guam to look for Stephen. She said declared dead or not, he's still just missing."

"Anna Lee, Hilton is dead."

"No!" It was more scream than statement. Not Hilton on that cold, hard table. She began sobbing. "Oh, Mama, no. Hilton can't die."

"We all die someday. I don't know how Robert will stand this."

Despite the inheritance they were due, Estelle took no pleasure in Hilton's death. It nearly killed her own husband. Robert was like a man without his senses. He raved and ranted and cried. At last people knew Robert Owens could cry. He couldn't even go to the funeral.

Estelle was afraid to leave him alone and didn't consider going to work. Johnn was worried about Robert too and encouraged her to stay by his side. He was surprised though to find that he'd come to depend on her. He really missed Estelle.

The doctor came every day for two weeks and sedated Robert. Anna Lee stared wide-eyed, and Estelle wrung her hands. Robert came down with hives, then boils, and finally blood poisoning. Estelle didn't dare voice her fears, but it was almost like Robert wanted to join Hilton, not go on living. Just when things could be so good for them.

Anna Lee had her own views. "Mama, do you think God is punishing Daddy?"

"What? Why would God be punishing your daddy?"

"Everyday he's got something else. He's like Job."

"Job wasn't being punished. God was testing him."

"You don't think boils and all that stuff wasn't punishment? Sometimes I wonder about God."

"Watch your mouth, Anna Lee Owens. That's sacriligious. Don't bring more down on us than we have already. There's nothing to punish your daddy for anyway."

"Maybe for caring more for Hilton than his own brother."

"Mr. Hilton."

"He said I should call him Hilton."

"Well, he's not around to say anything about it, is he?"

Estelle tried to deny the Job-like quality she came to see in Robert herself. Finally one morning she went to Robert and told him Mrs. Richards wanted to see him. Bearded and dirty, he sat up in bed.

Hilton's mother stood straight as an arrow and her hair was as smooth and neat as ever. "Robert, will you please go with me to the reading of Hilton's will? I could ask Heather to take me, but I'd rather it be you. You and Hilton were like brothers."

"That's the least I can do for Hil, Miz Fields. When do we go?"

"Nine tomorrow morning."

"I'll pick you up at eight forty-five." When she left, Robert got out of bed, shaved, and bathed. Just like that he snapped out of it. He told Estelle that as soon as the will was read he'd be on the road. "Lord help, I don't know how I'll ever catch up. Don't look for me home next weekend or any time soon."

At nine the next morning, Robert was sitting beside Mrs. Richards in the lawyer's office. Heather was already there, a black veil covering her face.

The lawyer finished reading the will before Robert realized his name had never been mentioned. Heather stood up, and Robert cleared his throat. "Excuse me, just a damn minute here, but did I miss something?"

The lawyer looked puzzled. "I beg your pardon?"

"I was to be beneficiary to a considerable amount of property. That was the agreement me and Hil had when I went to work for him."

"I'm sorry, Mr. Owens, but there is no mention of you. Mr. Fields left everything to his wife with the exception of a small bequest to his mother."

"But that's not possible. Hil wouldn't never of done me that a way. Never."

"Perhaps you had this agreement before Mr. Fields married."

"Yes, but . . . Hil wouldn't of done something like that without telling me."

"Obviously you're mistaken. Maybe he intended doing it at a later date. We wouldn't expect someone so young to die."

It took every ounce of strength Robert had to get Mrs. Richards home. He didn't say anything to her. Hilton hadn't talked to her about it. He knew that. Fireworks were going off in his head, but he walked her to the door, knowing he would never see her again.

Estelle was rinsing the coffeepot when he got home. "I thought you were going on the road."

"Not any more I ain't. Oh, I'm going on the road all right, but it's to find me another job."

Estelle dropped the coffeepot. "What do you mean?"

"I mean I've been taken for a fool. I thought Hil cared for me like I did him, but I was wrong. He was a lying fool, and I never want his name mentioned again. NEVER! He didn't leave me a damn thing after all he promised."

Estelle sat down, hard. "Why, Robert, after all your work . . ." She began to cry.

"Shut up, Estelle, you ain't got time to cry. We're leaving Bay Harbor. I'll find me a job in Tallahassee. That's where I belong anyway."

"But you and . . . well, you were boys there together."

"Boys, yes, not men with false promises. God, how could the bastard do me this way. It ain't the money. I thought he cared about me. I'll never get over this as long as I live."

He went to the bedroom and started dragging clothes out of the closet.

When Anna Lee came home from school there were boxes in all the rooms. Everything was turned upside down.

"What's wrong? Is there a hurricane coming?"

"I wish to God it was a hurricane. We're moving, that's what," her mother said tearfully. "We're wiping the dust of Bay Harbor off our feet."

"What are you talking about, Mama? Why? What do you mean, we're moving?"

"Just what I said. Your daddy's been tricked. He can't hold his head up in this town any more. He doesn't want to drag his name through the mud, us being a laughing stock. Start getting your things together. We got nearly our whole lives to go through in this house."

"NO! I don't know what you're talking about. I WON'T GO! You can't make me." Anna Lee began crying and Estelle jerked her by the arm and took her into the bathroom where she told exactly what had happened. She didn't tell her where they were moving. Robert didn't want anyone to know that, not even his daughter.

"Now straighten up. Your daddy's had all he can stand. Don't add to it. You'll kill him."

Anna Lee didn't give up without a fight. She was determined to stay in Bay Harbor. She went through the motions of packing but left the house every chance she got. First she went to her Uncle Johnn and begged him to let her stay and live with him and Miss Amy.

"We'd love to have you, darling, you know that, but after what's happened, you know we couldn't do that to your daddy. Heather is real indignant and is telling anybody who'll listen that your daddy thought he was coming into an inheritance. Robert feels like everybody in town's laughing at him. And then if you stayed behind . . . we couldn't do that."

She went to Helen. She even appealed to Virginia Edwards who had Lola's empty room just setting there. But the whole town knew what had happened to Robert Owens. They knew of the betrayal, and no one would take her in. No one.

A truck came to move them, and Anna Lee didn't think she could stand it.

"But it's my birthday. We can't leave on my birthday."

"Hush, Anna Lee, don't make this any harder on your daddy than it is already. This could kill him."

"Where's my necklace? I couldn't find it."

"What necklace?"

"The one Hilton gave me for my birthday last year."

Estelle gasped. "You are not to ever utter that name again. I don't know anything about your necklace. The truck's leaving. Get in the car and keep your mouth shut. It'll be hard enough for your daddy to drive without you yammering in the back seat."

"Y'all dust your shoes off before you get in the car." Robert stomped his shoes on the running board.

Estelle sat on the edge of the seat and bumped her shoes together. "This some new rule you just made?"

"We're shaking the dust of Bay Harbor from our feet. We're never coming back."

Anna Lee rubbed her shoes hard in the soft grey powder and pretended to shake them. "Some birthday," she muttered.

"I warned you, Anna Lee. Just because you're fourteen, you're not too old to switch. Here, take this." Estelle handed her some water in a little collapsible cup and dropped a white pill in her palm.

"What's this for?"

"Just take it. It'll make you feel better."

"No ma'am, it won't."

"Don't sass me. I want to see you swallow it. Your Uncle Johnn wanted it for you special."

"That doesn't sound like Uncle Johnn."

"I don't care what it sounds like, take it. Does your daddy have to stop the car and use his belt before we even get out of the city limits?"

The water tasted of metal, but Anna Lee swallowed the pill and didn't wake up until the next morning, asleep in her own bed in a small, hot house in Tallahassee, Florida. She wouldn't sleep that well again for twenty-five years.

Mrs. Richards lived only a little less than three months longer than her son. She didn't wake up one morning. Annie found her in bed. Dr. Mason called Heather, but she didn't even pretend grief. They had never been close before Hilton died and afterwards. . . Well, it all fell apart. Mrs. Richards never bought Heather's account of what happened the day Hilton collapsed. Never bought it for one minute.

Heather tried only once to befriend her mother-in-law, but the effort backfired. Mrs. Richards had sensed a coldness in Heather she'd never mentioned to her son. She knew she had no right count it as a fault. She was no stranger to the condition herself, and it was easy for her to spot the falseness in Heather's attempt to be friendly. "Don't patronize me, Heather, please." That's all she said.

"You needn't worry, Mrs. Richards, I have no intention of patronizing you ever again." After that day Heather didn't set foot in her mother-in-law's house until the morning of Dr. Mason's call.

Heather lost no time in putting the house up for sale. Tongues wagged when Heather opened the front door of that very private residence and invited the town inside. Everything was for sale. Heather didn't need the money. She wanted vengeance.

People who never expected to see the inside of this stately home opened drawers and chests and cupboards and helped themselves. Closet doors swung open to clothes that still held the fragrance of Mrs. Richards' perfume. They even took her shoes, exposing Mrs. Richards' very soul and gutting her privacy. No one paid any attention as trucks drove across the manicured lawn and up to the door to haul the furniture away.

Tyler Rose couldn't help herself. She had to go, all the while hating herself for the ghoulish feeling it gave her.

"Dear Tyler," Heather said sweetly, "some memento perhaps?"

Flustered, Tyler replied, "I . . . I don't know." She looked around her at the people shoving and grabbing everything they could, as though Heather might ask them to leave at any minute.

"Perhaps you'd like a picture of Hilton?"

"I'd like a picture of Hilton," someone said.

Tyler swung around to see Virginia Edwards standing behind her.

Heather smiled at Virginia. "Oh, I'll bet you would like a picture. It's funny that I haven't seen you since before the funeral. After all, I understand you were with Hilton when he died. They said you were alone with him. Silly me, I couldn't help but wonder if you were responsible for his death. What could you have said to him?"

Virginia gasped and paled momentarily. Then it was her turn to smile. She raised her voice an octave. "Well, I surely didn't tell him that you were barren, that Dr. Mason said you'd never had a child."

Tyler nearly fainted and caught hold of Virginia's arm to steady herself. Aunt Mary had confided that bit of information to her, and she'd told Virginia in strictest confidence. The only other person she'd told was Hilton when he was in a coma, her hope that it would give him the will to live and have his marriage to Heather annulled.

"How dare you come here and speak to me that way, spreading lies!"

"No lies, Heather. You know better." Virginia turned and snatched a picture of Hilton from an end table. "Thanks, Heather, I'll be on my way. Come on, Tyler, let's get out of this madhouse."

Virginia and Tyler went by the drugstore and ordered coffee. Tea no longer seemed so sophisticated. When they left, Tyler went by her dad's office. He'd moved his law books and things into the small room and planned to get an office in town soon. This news hadn't pleased her mother the way she thought it would, but he had a small practice going and was trying to extricate himself from the townspeople who didn't want him to give up his role as historian of their lives.

Larry turned when Tyler came in the door. "Are you okay? You don't look well."

"It was horrible, Dad, seeing people going through Mrs. Richards' things. They were like vultures. Heather hadn't touched a thing. It was all there just like Mrs. Richards left it that last night she went to bed. And I'd told Virginia Edwards something in confidence that she repeated to Heather right there in front of everyone."

Larry sighed. "I wouldn't worry about it. After all Heather's been through, I guess it can't have bothered her too much."

"I think it bothered her all right."

"Oh?"

"Yes. Virginia said loud enough for everyone to hear that Heather was barren. She'd never had a child."

Larry stood up suddenly, overturning his chair. "What? You can't be serious! Heather came here, came to me to bury her baby's ashes."

"I am serious. Aunt Mary slipped up and told me a long time ago. She didn't mean to, and I promised I'd never say anything, but then I slipped too and told Virginia."

"You knew that all this time? You're sure?"

"If you'd seen how upset Aunt Mary was to have told me, you'd know it was true."

Larry continued staring at Tyler for some moments and then walked out of the room and across the street, not even looking for cars.

Tyler heard a horn blow and saw a car swerve to miss him. "So that's how it is," she whispered. She turned back and began opening desk drawers. One was locked, but she found the key under a small piece of pink marble in the shape of a rose. Inside she found a worn letter. The creases had been folded and refolded through countless readings.

CHAPTER
Twenty-One

September 1947

Had they not left, Anna Lee would be starting high school in Bay Harbor soon, and she was frightened by the prospect of a strange school where she didn't know anybody. There were dark circles under red-rimmed eyes, but she couldn't do anything about that. It was the nightmares. They began after they moved to Tallahassee. Every night she fought to stay awake, knowing what waited beyond sleep.

Hilton Fields' car eased into town quiet as a dream, dark as a hearse. It was late, and the streets of Bay Harbor were deserted. Fog crept in from the Gulf of Mexico and dimmed his headlights with webs of angel hair. Hilton was coming back from the dead. No, that wasn't it. World War II had ended, and Hilton, lean and fit, perfect as a mannequin, was coming to see his closest friend, Robert Owens. He smiled at the thought.

Robert and his wife, Estelle, were asleep, but their young daughter, Anna Lee, was awake, listening for the car. She knew Hilton had arrived, and she had to stop him before he reached their house. Still in her nightgown, she ran out the front door on dream-weighted feet. "Stop," she tried to shout, but the dream choked her. "Oh, please stop."

She always woke up with her face wet with tears, one word on her lips. Stop. From the first she understood the dream's meaning. Over the years, it ceased to be an overriding issue in her life, but in times of stress it would surface again and never ceased to frighten her.

By the time they left Bay Harbor, Estelle had become a chain smoker, one cigarette after another. Anna Lee woke each morning to a chorus of wracking coughs from her parents.

Her Uncle Johnn bought their house and put it up for sale so they had money to get by until her dad found a job. It didn't take long. The irony was that he became night watchman at a bank. To make ends meet, her mother found work in the cafeteria at Florida State University, and Anna Lee babysat every chance she got. Times had never been so lean, not even during the war.

She missed Tyler and Lola. What had become of them? Her family couldn't afford a phone, and if there were letters she never saw them.

Her Uncle Johnn and Miss Amy visited from time to time, but they were forbidden to talk of Bay Harbor. Had it been possible, she knew her dad would have erased Bay Harbor from the map and her memory. He did what he could though.

"Baby, don't ever go back," he'd pleaded. "I may never ask you to do anything for me again, but I'm begging you, don't ever go back there as long as you live."

"But why . . ." she started when he interrupted.

"Maybe it's pride or remberin' the ridicule. I don't know. Maybe it's hurt, but I cain't stand the thought of any of us going there again. Ever. A part of me died back there in Bay Harbor. I'd spent a lifetime building a good name that was dragged through the mud."

"Oh, Daddy, people didn't blame you," she'd begun but he stopped her again.

"And don't go handing me any of that crap about the vessel that holds the hate. At my age that hate's the only thing I got left to hold on to. It's as sharp and hurtful as the day it rose up and bit me."

There'd been no reasoning with him. Anna Lee felt sure she could have returned without him finding out, but she could never bring herself to do it. She had her own fears of being seen, of being measured. And what if their disgrace had been her fault? She grew rigid with the memory of her voice saying unkind things to Heather, of the haunting guilt of her spying. Goose flesh crept up her arms, and she saw herself crouched beneath Larry Rose's window, spying on him and Heather, never dreaming Heather would become Hilton's wife, someone with the power to hurt her. How had she ever had the nerve to do some of the things she had, to read Heather's letter to Larry, left folded and worn in his desk! She never imagined the consequences her actions might have on her life and her family's.

And always, in the back of her mind, not frightening but most hurtful, Bay Harbor had gone on without her. She'd have no claim, no role to play.

She knew her mother was the unhappiest of all, going through the motions of a life with no joy in it, hating the work in the cafeteria at Florida State. In Tallahassee the cute college girls got the drugstore jobs. They had no need of Estelle's talent for decorating windows.

First Estelle soothed herself with smoking more and more cigarettes and later, alcohol. She went to bed drunk every night. It didn't take long for her mind to begin careening down the slippery slope of dementia. Cigarettes burned holes in the furniture throughout the house. She forgot how to crochet. There was no question of her working any more. Anna Lee took a part-time job after school, and life became even harder.

Estelle lived another year before it was all over. Robert blamed Hilton for that too. "He killed her as sure as if he'd put a bullet through her heart."

After that the years passed in a blur. Her Uncle Johnn insisted he sold their house for more than he expected and used the money to put Anna Lee through Florida State. Her dad aged more rapidly than seemed normal, and though Anna Lee hadn't thought it possible, grew more bitter. With scholarships and help from her Uncle Johnn, she went to graduate school at the University of Florida, having made arrangements for a widow to come live in the house and care for her dad. Four more years and he was so weak he couldn't go to Anna Lee's wedding. She and Joel, her Ramblin' Wreck from Georgia Tech, went to a Justice of the Peace with Johnn Owens and Amy their only attendants.

1971

Anna Lee's mother had been dead twenty-two years when the phone rang one evening. She could hear Joel speaking softly to someone and then, "Anna Lee, it's your Uncle Johnn." She broke into a big grin and rushed to take the receiver as Joel whispered, "bad news."

She couldn't keep the tremor from her voice, "Uncle Johnn, is anything wrong?"

"Just old age catching up with your dad. It's really bad. I'm at Tallahassee Memorial with him now. Do you think you could get here in a hurry?"

"I'm halfway there. Give me the room number, and I'll head to the airport for the first flight I can get."

It was still dark when she kissed Joel good-by and boarded the silver bullet she hoped would end her nightmare forever.

The sun had come up, and Anna Lee looked out the clouded window of the plane as it slowed for its descent into twenty-four years of loss and hurt.

She strained to see the familiar Florida landscape come into focus. As the plane reversed, it could have been gravity or memories that forced her back against the upright seat. A few more hours and she'd be home, though home had become a metallic taste on her tongue.

She could still feel the cold plastic of the phone against her ear, Uncle Johnn's plea to hurry. She might long for a small beach town, but the trees and landscape below her belonged to Robert Owens. Tallahassee was his youth, his home. The last time she'd seen him, he cried when he told her about going out into the woods one day some years before. He'd known those woods like the back of his hand. He owned that memory. She knew he'd been there with Hilton when they were young and wondered if he was thinking of that too.

"I got lost, baby. Lost in a place I knew as well as my own body. My truck was on the side of the road, close to where our old house had stood. They had to send someone to lead me out." He'd rubbed his sleeve against his eyes. "How many times can you be betrayed and go on living? Those woods had been mine, but not any more. It's tough gettin' old and losing all the things you love."

She'd tried to console him, all the while wondering why he couldn't understand that's what he'd done to her when he took her away from Bay Harbor. But he'd lost far more than his knowledge of a long ago forest. Time and grief had taken his humor, that wellspring of his personality. In many ways she'd lost her dad years before he'd die, and now she longed to have him back for just a little while, maybe a whisper of what he'd been when she was a child.

Anna Lee braced herself for multiple journeys. Her first stop was Tallahassee, home of her ancestors. She squeezed her eyes against tears that blurred her vision, tears that were for Robert Owens and herself, for all the years of missing the daddy he'd once been. And always and ever tears for Bay Harbor and people she loved.

Her second journey, the drive from Tallahassee to Bay Harbor, couldn't be measured in miles, only hurt. All she had of her former life was a small jar of sugar sand she'd scooped from the beach her last day there.

The plane pulled her into its descent. The anticipation of returning home, of being released from the long-held promise to her father, was marred by anxiety she tried to subdue. She couldn't hide forever from the answers Bay Harbor might give her. But her dad had answers too. Would he admit he'd been disappointed in her? That was part of the guilt she carried. She'd never been a son to follow him into the woods, to find him when he was lost. She knew he'd missed that. He'd been betrayed from the start by a nosy little daughter who might have caused his downfall.

She felt the thud of the wheels hitting the tarmac, and her stomach lurched with the forward motion of the plane. She continued facing the window until a stewardess bent over her and asked, "Miss, are you okay?"

"I'm fine, thank you."

"Do you have anything in the overhead?"

"No. Is there a problem?"

"We're in Tallahassee. You're the last person on the plane."

Anna Lee mumbled something about being distracted, but she didn't move. Her hands gripped the armrest. She closed her eyes and took several deep breaths. She should have let Joel come too. Dear sweet Joel. She felt guilty knowing he'd worry about her, but she'd waited so long, held in so much. She wanted this time for herself.

Anna Lee plucked a piece of lint from her Chanel suit, and made her way down the aisle and out of the plane into the glare of a Florida morning. She tucked a loose strand of hair into her French twist and kept her steps purposeful as she entered the terminal and made her way to the Hertz counter where she signed papers for a car.

She'd lived in Tallahassee until she was twenty-two, and while it still held an air of familiarity, it had never felt like home. She drove straight to the hospital where her Uncle Johnn was waiting just inside the door.

He pulled her to him. "I'm sorry, baby, he couldn't wait. Robert's on that final journey home."

She cried then. It hurt more than she'd expected.

"I'll go to the funeral home with you so we can make the arrangements."

She looked at Johnn Owens, really looked at him, and realized he wore his age well, but age was a bell tolling for all of them.

"You don't have to do that, Uncle Johnn. This is hard for you too. You were brothers after all."

"Thanks, darling. I am tired. It's been hard."

"It's been hard for all the years you looked after us."

"Nothing has been harder than this though." He took an envelope from his pocket and tapped it against the side of his hand. "They held this for me at the post office. It's to your dad. From Heather. After all these years. Hard to believe, isn't it? I got it last Friday and intended to give it to him next week. Then the call came."

Anna Lee remembered the worn letter Larry kept in his desk and smiled bitterly. "Not really. Heather was fond of letters."

Anna Lee folded the thin envelope and put it in her purse before walking her uncle to his car. "Daddy wasn't a religious man, but I'll find someone to say a few words. Uncle Johnn, I'm going to Bay Harbor as soon as I make the arrangements."

"I hoped you would. He was my brother, but I never agreed with the way he kept you away from the only home you'd ever known. Let me know when the interment will be, and Amy and I will drive back to Tallahassee and meet you at the old family cemetery. Nothing but our kin and the wind in the pines there. Be a nice send-off."

"I'll let you know tonight."

Anna Lee had no trouble finding the mortuary, and when she parked the strawberry red Chevy in front, she experienced a twinge of embarrassment despite her black suit.

She stood beside the car and stared at the ivy covered brick walls that hinted of mold and tombstones, so different from what she'd grown up with in Bay Harbor where the antique timbers of Rose Funeral Home were the pale blue of a sun drenched sky. That revered structure had possessed a stateliness that was never taken for granted, nor the effort that kept it that way. More than the loveliest woman in town, Rose Funeral Home was a reminder that life and beauty are fleeting.

Anna Lee decided to have her dad cremated, refusing to acknowledge that they never discussed such a plan. No ghost gas for Robert Owens. She was her own person now, a thirty-eight year old woman making her own decisions. Robert Owens couldn't hold her back any longer.

When everything had been finalized, a somber, moss-faced man escorted her back through the maze of rooms and opened the front door. Sunlight rushed into the dark hall and recalled a memory. Anna Lee stopped.

"Is anything wrong?"

"I was just remembering a death tour."

"I beg your pardon?"

"When I was growing up a friend of mine lived above the funeral home, and for a dime he'd take you on a death tour."

"I can't imagine."

"That's because you didn't know T. J." She left him standing in the open door and didn't look back as she got in the car and headed southwest, away from landlocked Tallahassee.

CHAPTER
Twenty-Two

The drive to Bay Harbor felt too short and too long. Anna Lee put miles between her and Tallahassee's moss laden trees, between the dip and climb of green hills, her car a divining rod searching for the Gulf of Mexico. It was all so familiar, the road an arrow shot through stands of fragrant pines and scattered homes.

At Bristol she saw that the stained, algae covered bridge over the Apalachicola River had been replaced with a wider, cleaner version that seemed so much shorter than she remembered. She wondered if Bristol's claim to fame, the gopher wood tree— timber of Noah's ark—still grew there.

She was queasy with anticipation, yet she'd tried to delay the bittersweet drive that gave way to Bay Harbor's sun-washed streets and neighborhoods of palms and cottonwoods and magnolias.

Anna Lee slowed the car and stared hard at the unfamiliar buildings she passed. Sagging frame houses leaned toward squat buildings of white plaster, dulled and stained by hard times. In all her recollections of Bay Harbor she'd never imagined this gentle shabbiness. *Had it always been this way?*

Heather's letter beat like a heart inside her purse. Her own heart raced with a kind of terror. Was Heather's intent to tell her dad it had all been his daughter's fault? She eased the car onto the small parking lot and walked to the end of the pier, repaired and sturdy. She sat on a bench, rubbing her hand over the worn wood. She took the letter from her purse. England! So she'd gone home after all.

Dear Mr. Owens,

My mum always said what goes around comes around, and here I am, living proof. There's so much you don't know about me, and I won't bore you with the sordid details of a life gone wrong. All this time and now I can't hold it in any more.

You were Hilton's best friend and didn't deserve to be treated the way you were. You loved Hilton. I loved someone else. I came to Bay Harbor expecting a future that had never existed for me. I don't want to make excuses for myself. I was never above using people. Not even now.

I'm using you to clear my own conscience. Hilton did leave you that inheritance. Larry Rose used his considerable skills as a lawyer to alter the will for me. He loved me, you see. It was a matter of love all around.

I thought I loved him, but now I wonder even about that. I could have taken Hilton's money and married Larry if he'd ever agreed to divorce that cow of a wife, but he'd lied to me from the start when he said he wasn't married, and again later about divorcing his wife and marrying me. I told myself I was justified in doing what I did to Hilton, to you and to Larry.

Don't get your hopes up. I have no intention of settling any money on you. I just wanted you to know Hilton was a fine man and died keeping his word. I'm not asking for forgiveness. I don't need it now.

Most sincerely,
Heather Fields

Anna Lee looked away when she passed the street where she'd lived, stared open mouthed when she passed a small public library, something they hadn't had when she lived there. A few blocks farther and she made an illegal U turn, turned right and "cruised main." Unable to bear the changes that tore at her heart, she turned toward the beach road and drove along the Bay again, headed toward her Uncle John's house. He was semi-retired now, and she knew he and Miss Amy were waiting to hear from her. All these years and she still thought of his wife as Miss Amy. But she was an adult now, and the lovely Miss Amy an old woman.

Clouds of memories fogged her vision, and she kept her foot on the accelerator as she passed her Uncle John's house. She turned the car around again. Forget duty. She'd been dutiful all her life. She owed Larry Rose a visit. Heather had seen to that. But she wanted to see Tyler as well, the beautiful Tyler Rose with the slanting green eyes and long, straw colored hair. How would she look? Would she be fat like her mother? Would she still grieve for the lost Stephen?

In a few short minutes, years too late, Anna Lee knew that despite its run-down appearance, she was at Tyler's house, still on the corner across from Rose Funeral Home. As she stepped out of the car the heels of her shoes sank and ground on the sharp grains of sand. She looked down and didn't see Andrew Geller pumps. She saw small bare feet. She must have stood there a thousand times. She leaned over and picked up a talisman of gritty sand that she rubbed between her thumb and forefinger. She drew a deep breath, inhaling the breeze that blew off the Bay.

Like the funeral home, Tyler's house had been something of a showplace. Not any more. There were boards missing from the fence and the remaining pickets sagged and needed painting.

And what had become of the lush garden where pink and yellow and white roses wound through ornate trellises and long- stemmed tea roses bloomed in a fragrant rainbow of color? Tyler's mother won prizes with those flowers. Taking careful steps Anna Lee walked to the forlorn garden and cupped a withered yellow rose in her palm.

She closed her eyes and felt the telegram in her hand. There among the roses she'd handed Tyler a piece of paper that changed her life forever.

She looked toward the window where Tyler's mother had waved to her that day. Surely Tyler was a mother now or possibly a grandmother, though Anna Lee still saw the slender girl who walked with shoulders thrown back, her chin high as though she was bucking a strong wind. As it happened, she had been bucking tragedy.

The house and grounds were bare. There were no swings or toys to suggest children. She turned and looked at the funeral home, no longer a showplace either. It cried out for a coat of paint, for a taste of heaven. Its sheen, its respect, belonged to the past. Anna Lee had waited so long, only to realize her family wasn't the only one that had suffered. Bay Harbor, the people she'd left . . . she might have come for two funerals.

She was seized with a moment of panic. Surely Tyler . . .

She rushed up the steps and pressed her face to the dusty screen door. *"Tyler? Oh, Tyler!"*

Twenty-four years might have been yesterday. "Anna Lee? Oh, my God, Anna Lee!" Tyler came running out the door and grabbed her, laughing and crying at the same time. "Aren't you a sight for sore eyes!" She put her hand over her mouth. "I can't believe you're here." She hugged her again and then pushed her away.

"Why, Anna Lee, if you only knew how often I've thought about you. Your Uncle told me a little, but after all this time, you're finally back!"

"Same here, Tyler. I've wondered all these years . . . and you look great!" The long pageboy hair had been cut in a short becoming style and her olive complexion was smooth and taut. She wore tight black pants with boots, a low-cut blouse of creamy silk, and lots of jewelry. Anna Lee looked at her. "You mean to tell me you're dressed like this and you weren't expecting me!"

"Darlin', you know I have to give these old men something to dream about. Why, I'm the wickedest thing in town!"

Anna Lee laughed. "I'll bet you are."

"Come on inside this old mausoleum and let's have something to drink."

Anna Lee paused and looked toward the funeral home. "I miss the swinging sign. It makes me sad that it's gone."

"Get over it, sweetie. I'm the only thing in this town that swings any more." She reached back and took Anna Lee's left hand. "I see you aren't Anna Lee Owens now."

"Oh, but I am. I kept my maiden name. I couldn't help myself. After all we'd been through, it was like a badge or a medal I had to wear. I hurt so for Daddy, Tyler. We had some terrible times."

"Your husband didn't mind your not taking his name?"

"A little, but he understood. Joel Saunders is a generous and loving husband. Oh, Tyler. I'm so lucky. I don't know what I ever did to deserve such a fine man."

"Well, darlin', you deserve a fine man if anybody does, but you'll always be Anna Lee Owens to me anyway. You know, sometimes when the light is just right and the fog rolls in, I swear I can see you running up the sidewalk toward my house."

"Sometimes I feel like I've never left, that I'm caught in that house some place. Still in Bay Harbor. I wish I had time to walk by after dark and look inside. I can't believe I wouldn't be there staring out the screen door."

"Who's to say you aren't?"

"Tyler, I can't stay. Daddy died last night. I've been in Tallahassee making the arrangements. Actually, I stopped to see your dad."

"Well, thanks a lot, but come on inside."

The house Anna Lee remembered as bright and rose scented was dark and smelled stale. An old man slept on the sofa. Tyler whispered, "Daddy had a stroke."

Anna Lee couldn't move for a moment, staring at the once handsome man who'd been so good to her. She looked at his slack mouth and sickly gray pallor. She'd find no answers there, but she kneeled beside the sofa.

Tyler stood in the kitchen door and called, "Anna Lee? How bout a glass of iced tea?"

"Thanks, but I can't really, Tyler. I just wanted to see your dad. He'd always been so good to me."

"Okay then. Let me turn the kettle off before I burn the damn thing up. Daddy does enough of that."

"Mr. Larry?"

He turned his head toward her, his eyes dimmed and rheumy. "How could you, Mr. Larry? How could you! I loved you. I realize that now. I loved you." She wanted to slap him, bang on his chest, anything to make him feel, to hurt him, to hate him.

Tyler came back. "Want to sit on the porch a bit and visit like old times?"

Anna Lee stood up and started out the door. "I have to head back to Tallahassee, some more arrangements to make and all."

She could feel the chill of Tyler's voice when she said, "Well, I'm sorry about your dad. Nice of you to stop by." She pulled the screen door closed and went back inside as Anna Lee went to the car. Cold with fury Anna Lee muttered to herself, *Don't judge me, Tyler Rose!* The wheels squealed as she turned the car around and headed toward the cemetery.

She didn't have to look for it. T. J.'s monument towered over everything else in the cemetery. Nothing less than a monument. The stone was white as alabaster, gently curved at the top with recessed stone forming a frame. Below was the image of a child, seen from the back. It was T. J. all right. Skinny and barefoot, he wore a T-shirt and shorts. Where his shoulder blades would have been the shirt bulged with the suggestion of sprouting wings. His hair was ruffled as though someone's hand had just passed through it, and his right hand was raised, index finger pointing skyward, indicating a point being made. He stood on his toes, poised to move, and at his feet mica and fools gold had been imbedded in the stone, sparkling like stars or a scattering of dimes.

"What a tribute, T. J. You must love it. I guess everything in this whole town is about love or the backside of love – hate. I've never quit missing you, you know. You got the worst deal of all, worse than any of us. I'll give the devil his due though. Your Uncle Larry did right by you." She reached in her purse and dropped several dimes at his feet before walking with bent head back to a red car that seemed to mock her.

She laid her head on the steering wheel and thought, *To thine own self be true.* She stopped briefly at her Uncle Johnn's and then headed toward the highway and Tallahassee. She wanted to go by her house, wanted that more than anything, but she couldn't do it. She couldn't stand any more hurt, and she loved that house. Without even realizing it, she found herself in front of Tyler's house instead.

Tyler was sitting in the swing. "Well, look what the cat dragged up. Remembering your manners?"

"What? Oh, I'm sorry, Tyler. I've had a couple of shocks today. I'm not myself."

"Well, that's good to know."

"I went by the cemetery."

"Beautiful, isn't it? Dad's masterpiece."

"It is."

"He gave you the credit, you know. Told everybody you were his inspiration."

"He did?"

"Yep. He retained some good qualities, Anna Lee."

"May I see him again?"

"Sure. He isn't going anywhere."

She knelt by the sofa. "Mr. Larry?" He turned toward her and she felt a glimmer of recognition in his eyes. "It's beautiful, Mr. Larry—T. J. would have been proud to know you cared so much."

He closed his eyes and a single tear coursed down his lined cheek.

She kissed his forehead and went out the front door.

"Bye, Tyler."

"That's it? What's it been? Twenty-four, twenty-five years and it's just 'bye'?"

"I'm sorry. That's all I'm capable of right now, but I'm thinking maybe I'll buy the old home place and use it for a vacation home. Come back and do right by you."

"You'll have to bargain with Lola for it then."

"What? Why Lola? I didn't know she was around here any more."

"She's most definitely around here, in your house, in fact. She owns it."

"In MY house?" Anna Lee hated the way her voice rose.

"Yep, your old homestead."

"I can't believe it."

"Well, you better believe it. Think she divorced her husband and looks like she's here to stay."

"But in my house!"

"Welcome home, baby girl."

"Oh cut the crap, Tyler."

"Well that's more like it, Anna Lee. Where's that spunk, that smart mouth that used to get you in trouble?"

"Right where it always was. And I'll tell you one thing. I'm coming back, Tyler. Just you wait, I'll be back. Lola, of all people."

ABOUT
the Author

Write about what you know, what you love—that's why Ruth Coe Chambers writes about Florida. So that time and distance would not steal the memories of her hometown, Port St. Joe, she created *The Chinaberry Album* to secure its place in history. In addition to stand-alone works such as *The Chinaberry Album*, its sequel *Heat Lightning*, two prize winning plays, and other upcoming surprises, her work has garnered accolades in literary competitions and has appeared in print, online magazines, and essay anthologies. She continues her writing, immersively exploring the sandy, salty fabric of Florida.

Made in the USA
Charleston, SC
26 September 2015